D0191914

"An afternoon spent with Minerva was such frivolous fun that one would like to spend the next five with Annabelle, Deirdre, Daphne, Diana, and Frederica."

The Witchita Eagle-Beacon, Witchita, Kan.

"Readers will ache for Minerva as she becomes the subject of London wagers and cheer as she begins to accept, and then pursue, her own desires. . . . Had Jane Austen written more openly about sex, she would have penned Minerva's story."

Boston Herald

"A TREASURE TROVE!"

Rocky Mountain News

"The book is witty and the characters are well-drawn."

Library Journal

"THE BRIGHTEST AND BEST OF TODAY'S REGENCIES."

The Kirkus Reviews

MINERVA

Marion Chesney

FAWCETT CREST • NEW YORK

A Fawcett Crest Book
Published by Ballantine Books

Library of Congress Catalog Card Number: 83-10931

ISBN: 0-449-20580-0

This edition published by arrangement with St. Martin's Press

Manufactured in the United States of America

First Ballantine Books Edition: August 1984

For Barbara Lowenstein
With love

TO MINERVA
(from the Greek)

My temples throb, my pulses boil,
I'm sick of Song, and Ode, and Ballad—
So, Thyrsis, take the Midnight Oil,
And pour it on a lobster salad.

My brain is dull, my sight is foul,
I cannot write a verse, or read—
Then, Pallas, take away thine Owl,
And let us have a lark instead.

Thomas Hood

Chapter One

Up until the winter of 1811, anyone would have described the vicar of St. Charles and St. Jude, the Reverend Charles Armitage, as a very happy man.

He had six beautiful daughters and two fine sons. He had a pallid, ailing wife whom he largely ignored, and above all, he had his hunters and his hounds. He was a jolly, robust, shovel-hatted man who rode to hounds in a pepper and salt coat and was welcome at the dinner tables of almost every house of note in the county of Berham.

Admittedly, Sundays were apt to be a bit of a trial when he took his sore head and heartburn into the pulpit to read the sermon his eldest daughter, Minerva, had dutifully prepared for him.

But the other days were splendid, taken up with the chase, the gun and the rod.

His parishioners were used to the vagaries of their vicar, and only a few of the more devout occasionally longed for a vicar who cared more for the word of God than for the word of the *Sporting Chronicle* and *Bailey's Guide to the Turf*.

He owned two farms from which he derived much of his income. He had turned a deaf ear to any suggestions of using modern methods of agriculture, and that, combined with a

succession of quite dreadful harvests, had left the vicar in a
difficult financial situation by the winter of 1811. Added to
that, his two sons, the twins, Peregrine and James, were
shortly to celebrate their ninth year. They were largely untu-
tored, and the vicar was overcome with a burning desire to
send them to Eton, which would involve a year for both at
Dr. Brown's crammer in the King's Road, London, first, to
ensure that they passed their entrance exams.

His money seemed to have melted like fairy gold. Had his
concern for the boys' education been motivated by any altru-
istic thoughts, then perhaps he might not have hit on an idea
to raise himself out of the mire of debt into which he had
fallen. But he was a totally self-centred man, and he saw the
boys as an extension of himself, young bear cubs to be
licked into the Armitage image. And so he set about
schemes for raising money with all the single-minded zeal of
the true egotist.

His first thought was to pay a visit on his brother, the baronet, at the Hall.

Sir Edwin Armitage, Bart, looked down his long nose at
his brother, the vicar, considering him boorish and uncouth.
Social intercourse between the two families was somewhat
strained. Sir Edwin had a great deal of money and two proud
daughters and a proud wife. He would have severed all con-
nection with the vicar had not his wife pointed out to him
that it was their Christian duty to be kind to "those poor Armitages," which, being translated, meant that Lady Edwin
and her daughters gained much pleasure from dressing in
their best and contrasting their finery with the plain, shabby
frocks of the Armitage girls.

But the Reverend Charles Armitage was determined to get
money from his brother, and so he knew he would have to
toady quite dreadfully.

"Edwin is a *put*, Edwin is a *snob*, Edwin is a *chaw-
bacon*," he muttered to the tune of his hunter's hooves as he
rode through Hopeworth towards the Hall, the entrance of
which was situated at the far end of the village.

There was a hard, sparkling frost on the ground. It would
have cut the hounds' paws which is why the reverend was
not out hunting. It also accounted for his morose temper.

A pale, thin disc of a sun, not enough to warm the frigid air, swam through a haze of cloud. "I must have the money, I must have the money," went the vicar's litany. "Oh, my hounds and horses. Oh, Bellsire and Thunderer, oh, Rambler and Daphne," he went on, going over the names of his hounds to comfort him.

Hopeworth was a pretty village with trim cottages and neat gardens. A sheet of ice like a looking glass covered the village pond on the green, and women in shawls were huddled around the well. From the Six Jolly Beggarmen, Hopeworth's public house, floated an aroma of beer and brandy and rhubarb. He contemplated dropping in for a glass of shrub to fortify himself, and then decided against it. Better to get the distasteful business over as soon as possible.

The Hall was a handsome, Baroque, red-brick mansion, built in 1725. To the north and east of it stretched well-wooded parkland. The Saloon into which the vicar was ushered held an agreeable mixture of English, French and Dutch furniture. There were Louis XVI armchairs covered in Beauvais tapestry, and some fine lattice-backed Chippendale chairs. The walls were covered with hand-painted Chinese wallpaper.

"I will h'ascertain whether the master is at 'ome," said the fat footman.

"Cockney popinjay," said the vicar, but he did not say it aloud. He had no wish to waste time putting his brother's servants in their place.

He fought with his temper as the minutes ticked away and his brother did not come. The vicar strode up to the mantelpiece and straightened his stock. He suddenly felt that it might have been better to don morning dress for this money-eliciting occasion instead of an old-plush game coat with many pockets, gosling-green cords and very dark tops.

A genteel cough from behind made him swing around. Sir Edwin and Lady Edwin had entered the room.

Both were tall and stately and impeccably dressed. Sir Edwin followed the Brummell fashion, the skirts of his blue coat being cut back to form a square-cut tail coat with pockets in the pleats. The sleeves were gathered and padded

{ 3 }

to give the "kick-up" effect. His shirt collar was so high and so starched he had difficulty in turning his head.

He wore high-waisted, canary-yellow, stockinette trousers and thin slippers trimmed with small buckles. His gray hair was back-combed into a high mass on top of his head with curls over the temples. He was as thin as the vicar was stocky. Where the vicar's face was round and ruddy, the baronet's was thin and pale. The vicar had twinkling little shoe-button eyes embedded in pads of fat. The baronet's were a washed out blue colour with a peculiarly blue iris which gave him the blind look of some classical statues of the eighteenth century.

Lady Edwin was also tall. Her face would have been thin had she not transformed it with wax pads worn inside the cheeks to give the Dutch doll effect which was going out of fashion. This also gave her speech a muffled, strangled sound, which was the envy of every woman in the village with aspirations to gentility.

She was wearing a high-waisted, vertical gown with a high neck and deep muslin ruff. The hem, which was untrained and fashionably short to expose most of the foot, was trimmed with Spanish embroidery. She wore her brown hair short and frizzled on the front.

"Well, well," said the vicar heartily. "It's nice to see you, brother . . . ma'am." He jerked a bow in Lady Edwin's direction.

Sir Edwin looked out of the window to where the ornamental lake glittered palely under its coating of ice.

"Too hard to go hunting, Charles," he said in his dry, precise voice. "You must be at loose ends. I gather that is the reason for your visit."

"Not at all! Not at all!" said the vicar, nervously, rubbing his large, square hands. "I wondered how you went on. How are Josephine and Emily?" Josephine and Emily were the baronet's daughters.

"Blooming, quite blooming," said Lady Edwin with a doting smile. "Squire Radford was saying only the other day that they are the most beautiful girls in the county."

"Eyesight still as bad, heh?" said the vicar sympathetically. He did not pay much attention to his own daughters, leaving the eldest, Minerva, to look after the welfare of the other five. But he knew, for everyone had told him, that they far surpassed any female for miles around in looks. Even little eleven-year-old Frederica!

The bluff vicar did not mean to insult Lady Edwin. Josephine and Emily were whey-faced, long-nosed, giggling nonentities. Therefore, it followed that the Squire's eyesight must be worse.

Lady Edwin bridled and would have said something had not her husband motioned her to silence.

"I've got a terrible thirst on me," said the vicar hopefully.

"Sit down, Charles," said Sir Edwin. The vicar sat in a French armchair which groaned under his weight. The Baronet and his wife arranged themselves in chairs opposite. Sir Edwin rang the bell and ordered champagne.

"I say," said the vicar anxiously, "you ain't got any of that wine with the yellow seal?" The vicar detested champagne which he considered a drink fit only for the ladies.

"Very well," said Sir Edwin, folding his thin lips into an even thinner line. "A bottle of the best burgundy, James. Now Charles . . ."

Charles Armitage wriggled in his chair like a guilty schoolboy before the headmaster. "I'll come straight to the point," he said, taking out a large Belcher handkerchief and mopping his brow.

"It's like this. The harvests have been mortal bad . . ."

"I know," said the baronet with a superior smile. "But wheat is still fetching high prices. You should have put more of your land under wheat. The little you would have reaped last year would have fetched you more than these acres of Swedish turnips. Then I believe you were experimenting with Indian corn. Not a suitable crop for an Englishman."

"Be that as it may," said the vicar, "I've been hit hard and am in need of money."

"Then you must retrench," said the baronet severely. "A glass of wine, brother. I trust you will find it to your liking. Yes, retrench, that is the answer. May I point out that a sale of your hunters and hounds would considerably alleviate . . . ?"

"No, you may not," growled the vicar. "I am prepared to do without luxuries. But necessities must remain. I have spent my life line-breeding those hounds and now they're reckoned the best working hounds in England. They're fast but they're not massively boned, very stout, and very sorty."

"You are a parson," said Sir Edwin coldly. "You're supposed to have your mind fixed on higher things."

The vicar looked at him with the puzzled innocence of a child. What could be higher, what could be more spiritual, than the sound of a tally-ho! and the sight of the hounds straining after the scent on a wet November morning?

But he said, "I've got the boys to send to school, Edwin, and that's a mort o' money."

"I cannot find myself in sympathy with you at all," said Sir Edwin severely.

"Ho, you don't, do you?" muttered the vicar, pouring himself another glass of burgundy, knocking it back in one gulp, and giving a discreet belch.

"No, because you should have made provision for your family. Have you heard of Aesop?"

"Milksop?"

"No. Aesop. A-E-S-O-P," spelled the baronet crossly.

"Oh, some Greek ivory turner."

"Really, brother, I am not talking about a card sharp. I swear you learned nothing at Oxford."

"I pulled stroke-oar in the Christchurch boat," said the vicar hotly. And then, adding in a milder tone, for he still had hopes of wringing some money from his brother, "Go on about this here Greek."

"Aesop wrote a fable about the ant and the grasshopper," said Sir Edwin. "Fetch me that book over there, my dear. Listen and learn, Charles. Listen and learn."

He proceeded to read the fable of the grasshopper who had danced and sung all summer and then starved in the winter because it had neglected to pile up provisions, while the hard-working ant survived the winter by having the foresight to prepare for it.

"And the moral of that is," said Sir Edwin sententiously,

" 'it is thrifty to prepare today for the wants of tomorrow.' "

The vicar listened in bewilderment. He was a true countryman. Insects were insects, birds were birds, animals were animals. They didn't go around chatting and prosing on. But one thing did strike him.

"This here ant," he said cautiously. "It told that there grasshopper to go and sing and dance when the poor b . . . , saving your presence, ma'am, I mean insect, asked for a bit o' help?"

"Yes," said Sir Edwin smugly.

The vicar shook his head in amazement and fortified himself with another glass of wine.

Then he thought he had it and his face cleared.

"Oh, it's them *Greek* ants," he said triumphantly. "They're not British. You wouldn't get your British ant being so clutch-fisted."

"This is absolutely absurd," said Lady Edwin.

"I quite agree," said the vicar. "So to get back to the matter in hand . . ."

"What I am trying to point out to you, brother, is that we have made provision for our daughters. They both have excellent dowries and will marry well, and the fortunes that they marry will be added to our fortune. I think I must leave you to face the consequences of your own folly. If, however, you should consider selling your pack . . . ?"

"Never!" said the vicar.

"In that case, brother, if you have quite finished . . . ?"

The vicar rose and gathered his dignity about him.

" 'And why beholdest thou the mote that is in thy brother's eye, but considerest not the beam that is in thine own eye?' "

"My dear Charles . . ."

"Matthew, chapter seven, verse three," said the vicar, cramming on his hat. "Good day to you."

Lady Edwin's strangulated voice followed him out into the hall. "The only time that wretched man remembers any of his Bible is when he's trying to be nasty."

The vicar rode gloomily out of the grounds of the Hall and turned his horse in the direction of The Six Jolly

Beggarmen. He did not feel like company, and so he took his pint of shrub out to the bench in front of the inn, which was empty of occupants because of the cold weather.

He felt he ought to pray but found he could not. If he prayed anywhere off the hunting field, he had a picture of an anthropomorphic God with a long beard and shaggy eyebrows who was simply waiting up in the clouds for His attention to be attracted to the sinner so that He could send down some more shame and blame.

So the vicar thought instead about his large brood of children. Apart from the aforementioned twins and eleven-year-old Frederica, there was Diana, twelve, Daphne, thirteen, Deirdre, fourteen, Annabelle, sixteen, and Minerva, nineteen.

Minerva was the "mother" of the vicar's household. Mrs. Armitage was a professional invalid, lying all day long on the sofa in the vicarage parlour, surrounded by medicines and powders.

He thought angrily of Josephine and Emily. They would need to have a considerable fortune before anyone married one of them, he thought sourly. Now, take Minerva for instance. She was a small, dainty beauty. A bit strict. A bit severe. But a beauty for all that. Why, she could get married without a dowry!

The sun glinted palely on the ice of the pond. The vicar had the feeling that he was about to hit on a solution.

He was not an inveterate gambler. He had once tried putting a monkey on a horse at Newmarket which had fallen three yards down the course, and since then, he had carefully placed only small sums of money from time to time on those infuriating racehorses.

He sat drinking his shrub and waiting for that idea which was germinating somewhere in his brain to blossom into full glory. A black cloud blotted out the sun and with it the vicar's hopes of a solution faded.

His stomach rumbled. Minerva handled the household budget which meant the meals at the vicarage were sustaining, but hardly exciting.

It was three o'clock and dinner called. But dinner was to be neck of mutton.

Then he suddenly decided to call on the Squire and invite himself to the Radford table.

He should really call home first and tell them. But Mrs. Armitage knew of his mission and would learn of its failure and would promptly have a Spasm.

"Sufficient unto the day is the evil thereof," quoted the Reverend Charles Armitage. He mounted his horse and rode in the direction of Squire Radford's cottage *ornée* whose thatched roofs could be seen peeping above the trees on the other side of the village pond.

The following day was Sunday and the vicar was suffering from having drunk long and deep the night before.

He stood in the pulpit, hanging onto the wings of the brass eagle, and summoned up the strength to read the sermon Minerva had prepared for him. His mouth felt like the bottom of a parrot's birdcage and there was a dull pounding behind his temples.

His daughter had based the sermon on a text from Proverbs which struck her father as being wickedly apt.

" 'Look not upon the wine when it is red, when it giveth his colour in the cup, when it moveth itself aright.

" 'At the last it biteth like a serpent, and stingeth like an adder.' "

The vicar cast a reproachful look in the direction of Minerva who was sitting at the end of the Armitage family pew.

Minerva!

A shaft of sunlight was shining through the glass windows, lighting up Minerva's enchanting face, wide gray eyes, and soft pink mouth, straight little nose, thin arched brows, long, long lashes.

On her head she was wearing a close-fitting hat made of ribbons and flowers.

The vicar saw her for the first time as many men would see her.

That was it! Minerva!

The tight-fitting Kerseymere wool gown under the jaunty little spencer showed a generous bosom and a trim waist. Her ankles, he remembered with awe, were quite beautiful.

The Reverend Charles Armitage had a vision of heaven all in that moment. His daughter would marry a fortune, and his own days stretched out in front of him in a paradise of never-ending rainy Novembers where the scent was high and the hounds and horses fleet.

"Hoic, holloa! Hoic, holloa! Hoic, holloa!" yelled the vicar of St. Charles and St. Jude to the indifferent plaster cherubim at the roof.

"Bedlam," hissed Lady Edwin to her husband. "Definitely Bedlam. I see no other future for him."

The vicar's overworked curate, Mr. Pettifor, took over as he had done so many Sundays before.

The gentry tut-tutted in dismay. But the humbler folk of the village were moved. They thought the good vicar had really had a spiritual revelation, so transfigured had been his face.

Chapter Two

It is a sad fact that many Cinderellas are self-made rather than born that way, and such was the case of Minerva Armitage. Had she let loose the reins of the household, then it is possible that her Mama would have been forced to rise from her semi-sickbed and take charge. Had she not volunteered to write her Papa's sermons, then perhaps he would have studied his Bible more and William Taplin's *The Sporting Dictionary and Rural Repository* less.

Minerva had a fine intelligence and insufficient education.

She was energetic and restless, and unsatisfied with the dull country routine of a gentlewoman—and in order to offset this boredom, Minerva had set about devoting herself to her five sisters and two brothers.

As she grew older, it was she who bathed their hot foreheads when they had the fever, it was she who bandaged cuts and grazes, and it was she who visited the parishioners and ran the household. Each month of each year brought her new, self-imposed duties, and, as she grew in beauty, so did she grow in long-suffering. For, in truth, the fair Minerva had become a trifle priggish and smug.

Papa's announcement at dinner that Sunday that Minerva

was to make her come-out in London was met with shocked silence.

Then Mrs. Armitage had one of her Spasms and had to be brought round with the hartshorn and a quantity of feathers burnt under her nose. Annabelle, the nearest in age to Minerva, looked startled and then jealous. The boys looked surly and kicked the table legs and the other girls began to sob. Minerva had managed to spoil the whole family.

"What will we do without Merva?" wailed the younger ones. Merva was Minerva's nursery name.

"This is sudden and rather startling intelligence," said Minerva in a calm voice, although her heart was beating hard. "I have no reason to go to London. If you are thinking of marrying me off, I am young yet, and there are plenty of men in the county."

"None that are rich enough," said the vicar, taking a pinch of snuff. "Fact is, m'dear, we'll all be in the River Tick if you don't pull us out. All those bad harvests. The farms aren't supplying enough. The only alternative is to re-trench. And that means no school for you boys, no pretty dresses and gee-gaws and no," he added glaring at his wife, "no dosing yourself with all them patent medicines."

"Oh, will no one have pity on a poor, sick, old woman?" wailed the vicar's wife.

The members of the Armitage brood began to look at their eldest sister thoughtfully. And the more they looked, the more Minerva faded from her dining chair to be replaced by a sack of golden guineas.

"This is nonsense," said Minerva, with a sigh of relief. "Papa must be foxed!" He was already broaching his second bottle of port. "Papa is funning. If we have no money, then we cannot possibly afford all the horrendous expense of a Season."

"I ain't paying for it," said the vicar, fidgeting in his cavities with a goose quill. "Lady Godolphin will foot the bill and she'll get paid back every penny after you nail a rich husband."

"Lady Godolphin?"

"She's on your mama's side, sort of cousin thirteen times

removed. I ain't seen her this age, but she always had a soft spot for me.''

Minerva pushed back a stray black ringlet. "Annabelle," she pleaded, turning to her sister, "you are much prettier than I. Would not *you* like to go instead?"

Annabelle's big blue eyes sparkled with excitement, but before she could open her mouth, the vicar said, "Won't do. She's got yaller hair and yaller hair ain't the fashion. 'Sides, she's too young. Dark beauties is what they want. Minerva'll fetch 'em. And see here, Bella, if Minerva marries well, she'll bring *you* out, and Mrs. Armitage can go to all the fancy quacks in London, and the rest of you young ladies can eat all the sugar plums you want. Perry and James can go to Eton like they've always wanted and . . ."

His voice trailed away. The vicar could be quite stupid on occasion. Yet when he had set his heart on something, he would put forward every argument he could think of until he had got it.

"But I had not thought of getting married for some time," said Minerva. "If at all! I would like to stay here and be a support to you and Mama in your declining years."

"If you don't get us some money," said the vicar reasonably, "our years are going to decline unnaterel fast."

An infuriating pious look appeared on Minerva's pretty face. "Have you asked Him?" she asked, pointing upward.

"Yes, course I have," said the vicar cheerfully, "and you're His answer. So there!"

There was another silence while Minerva's large gray eyes flew from face to face. The children were guiltily thinking of what life would be like without Minerva. No more parsimonious meals. No endless washing and scrubbing of hands and faces. No moral readings from Mr. Porteous's sermons at bedtime. Peregrine and James had wanted to hunt, but Minerva had stopped them, saying they were too young. But now . . .

Annabelle was considering how she would shine as the prettiest girl in the county, with Minerva away. Perhaps she could flirt a little at the Hunt Ball without Minerva's cold reproving eye on her.

Mrs. Armitage was lost in a rosy dream of London doctors and London chemists with their delicious bottles of medicine, glowing in the candlelit windows like all the jewels of Aladdin's cave.

The vicar craftily tapped in the last nail in Minerva's coffin.

"I know this is hard on you, Minerva," he said, "but you must sacrifice yourself for your family. You must *martyr* yourself. Ah, me! It is indeed asking too much."

Minerva's eyes began to glow softly. She was needed by her family, as they had always needed her.

"I shall go, Papa," she said, throwing back her head, as if being sent to the guillotine instead of a round of dissipated pleasure.

"Good girl," said the vicar absent-mindedly. Having got what he wanted, he lost interest in Minerva. He would, of course, have to write that pesky letter to Lady Godolphin, but, after the reply, he could push his eldest out of the family nest in spring and wing her on her way to London.

Minerva forced herself to go about her duties that evening as if nothing world-shattering had happened.

The children wanted to use Minerva's prospective comeout as an excuse to stay up late, but Minerva said firmly that they must go to bed at the usual time. As a treat, she would read a story, especially for the boys, and the youngest girls might listen if they wanted.

The vicarage was a pleasant building with dining room, drawing room, parlour, and study on the ground floor, six bedrooms on the first, and the servants' rooms in the attics at the top. There were not very many servants. There was a cook-housekeeper who held sway in the kitchen. There was a housemaid who doubled as a parlour maid when company called, an odd-job man who doubled as a butler on grand occasions, John Summer who acted as groom, coachman, kennel master and whipper-in, a small knife boy who was also pot boy and boot boy and page, when the occasion demanded, and a woman who came daily from the village to do the heavy work.

The boys had a room to themselves. Mr. and Mrs. Armitage had separate rooms, and the six sisters shared the remaining three rooms, two sisters to each room.

Apart from Annabelle, who considered herself too old at sixteen for bedtime stories, the other children all piled into the boys' bedroom to hear Minerva's reading, hoping that this time it might be something a little more jolly than usual.

Their hopes were soon dashed as the tale began to unfold in Minerva's soothing, mellow voice.

It was a story about two schoolboys, one quiet and serious, who never told a lie, and the other one, tall and handsome, the scion of a noble house, good at games, dashing and handsome.

The serious one was called Claud, and the dashing one, Guy. This was admittedly a promising start. The boys promptly vowed Guy no end of a good fellow, and the girls were delighted and surprised at having a handsome hero featured in one of Minerva's bedtime tales.

But, alas, for the dashing Guy. They might have known he was not to be the hero. While he won cricket matches for his school, while he was fawned on and admired, while the serious and lowly Claud was despised, it was soon to be revealed that this fine exterior was nothing more than a "whited sepulchre."

"What's a whited . . . whatever you said?" demanded Perry.

"I know," said red-haired Deirdre, shyly. "It means someone is nice on the outside but all full of rotting, decaying things on the inside."

Minerva nodded, and the other girls shrieked in dismay.

"Not Guy!" they cried, having already begun to weave rosy fantasies about this storybook boy.

"Listen!" admonished Minerva, and read on.

Guy had sent Claud to his room to fetch his cap, since he was in the habit of treating even his peers as servants. While he was searching for Guy's hat, the meek Claud came across a Latin crib.

Guy, it appeared, had been sailing through all his Latin exams, because, with the crib, he already knew the English translation for everything.

"Well, I think he was jolly clever to memorize it all," said Perry hotly. There was a murmur of agreement.

"So what was Claud to do?" questioned Minerva, brightly ignoring the interruption.

They all looked at her in a baffled way since it had never crossed their minds that Claud ought to do anything.

Minerva shook her head in mock dismay and continued. Claud, it appeared, had done his duty by taking the crib directly to the headmaster and reporting that Guy had been cheating.

Guy was expelled from the school, a broken reed, all flamboyance gone, while Claud studied his uneventful way to modest glory.

"And the moral of that is," said Minerva, closing the book with a snap, "honesty is the best policy."

James, black-haired and blue-eyed like his twin, stared at Minerva, as if he could not believe his ears.

"You look horrified, James," smiled Minerva. "What would *you* have done?"

"I'd have taken that Claud-creature and drawn his cork," retorted James.

"I will not have cant spoken in this house," said Minerva severely.

But a chorus of young voices defended James.

"Claud's a sneak."

"Guy was a first-rater . . ."

"I hope Guy joined the army and became a general and . . . and . . . killed Boney."

"Into bed all of you," said Minerva sternly. "How am I to leave for London with a quiet heart if I know that you are all not morally sound?" She swept the girls out of the boys' bedroom, but not before she heard Perry mutter, "She's probably going to marry some wet fish like Claud—if she marries at all."

Minerva compressed her lips and did not deign to show that she had heard.

When the younger girls were tucked up in bed, she went to join Annabelle with whom she shared a room.

Annabelle was sitting at the toilet table, dreamily brushing out her long, golden hair.

At her sister's entrance, she paused with the brush in mid-air and studied her elder sister's quiet face.

"It's such a waste," sighed Annabelle, and fell to brushing again.

"What is?" came Minerva's voice from behind a lacquered screen. She would no more have dreamed of undressing in front of her sister than she would have dreamed of spitting in church.

"Your going to London," said Annabelle. "I don't know if you've ever thought of men at all?"

"In what way?" came Minerva's voice, muffled in cloth.

"In a romantic way," said Annabelle, putting down the brush and swinging around.

"Surely *you* don't think of men in that way?" came Minerva's infuriatingly amused voice from behind the screen. "You are much too young."

"I am sixteen," flashed Annabelle. "And I may tell you I think of little else."

"Then you should be improving the moral tone of your mind to prepare yourself to be a good and modest wife."

"I don't *want* to be married to the sort of man who wants a 'good and modest wife,' " said Annabelle. "I want a dashing and handsome Buck, a Fribble, a Corinthian, a Dandy. It's a wonder you haven't fallen for poor Mr. Pettifor!" Mr. Pettifor was the curate.

"It is indeed a wonder," said Minerva, appearing around the screen in her nightdress. "He is a fine young man, devoted to the duties of the parish."

"He has also a long red nose and a wet mouth and . . . ."

"Stop this instant," said Minerva. "What has come over you, Annabelle? You have not spoken thus before!"

"London," said Annabelle dreamily. "The walks, the rides, the routs, the balls, the opera. Almack's! How I should love it so! How I should like some beaux! It is so *dull* here. Nothing happens here and nothing ever will.

"Because you will *not* be married, Minerva. That saintliness of yours will offset your looks. Why, it makes you positively repellent!"

Large tears appeared in Minerva's eyes and slowly slid, unchecked, down her cheeks.

"Annabelle," she said in a choked voice. "I was assured we loved each other. Can I be mistaken?"

"No, no, Merva," sighed Annabelle. "I am a frightfully jealous cat, that is all. Please dry your eyes. We will say no more about it. I am quite fatigued. You do forgive me, don't you?"

And of course Minerva did. It was unthinkable she should do otherwise.

But she lay in bed a very long time, staring up into the darkness, long after Annabelle had gone to sleep.

Now that she was alone, or as alone as anyone could be who shares a bedroom, Minerva had to admit to herself that she was afraid. She knew that a heavy responsibility had been placed on her shoulders. She must marry, and marry well.

She was perfectly prepared to sacrifice herself for her family's happiness, since that was the only way she knew of being happy herself. Somewhere deep inside, Minerva did not really think much of herself, and so she needed to be needed. But she was sensible enough to realize that her appearance was not enough on its own to attract a suitable partner.

Her cousins, Josephine and Emily, worked at nothing else but the art of attracting men. Minerva had rather pitied them for this. Now she was faced with hard reality.

Surely she herself would now have to study those despised arts. Minerva wondered whether to pray for guidance, but her mind shrank from the idea almost as soon as it was formed.

Like quite a number of the human race, she prayed to a God in her own image. Since she was very hard on herself, she thought of God as a harsh judge, forever on the lookout to punish the slightest tottering step from the straight and narrow. He would surely not concern himself with the arts and foibles of the ballroom.

But surely there must be a man somewhere in the whole of London—and that meant London from Kensington Palace to St. James's—who would have high standards, solid values, who would assist her in the delicate job of training up the minds of the younger Armitages.

Before she finally fell asleep, she had conjured up just

such a man in her imagination. He would not be particularly handsome, but of a serious and sober frame of mind.

They would not dance much, but would prefer to sit quietly together, discussing weighty topics. Perhaps she might allow him to press her hand! But that delicious thought caused a wave of gooseflesh to run over Minerva's body and her conscience told her her thoughts were taking a decidedly sinful turn.

So she turned back to the serious discussion in the ball-room, and fell asleep, feeling more comfortable, than she had all evening.

Morning brought even more comfortable, sobering thoughts. The Season was still a long way away. This was November. The Season did not begin until April. And her family still needed her.

Perhaps Lady Godolphin would not want her. And then perhaps Papa might hit upon some other scheme for finding the Armitages money.

The boys were taught their lessons by the curate, Mr. Pettifor. The girls, with the exception of Annabelle, had to be made ready for school. They attended a seminary for young ladies in the nearby town of Hopeminster, and were conveyed each day, there and back, in the vicar's elderly and creaking travelling carriage, pulled by two of the plough horses.

Minerva hurried about, finding gloves and braiding hair, supervising the serving of breakfast, making sure the carriage had not been invaded by hens overnight, since the door of the carriage house was often left open by mistake, thereby allowing families of hens and geese to use the carriage as a sort of coop.

Finally, all four young girls were packed into the carriage, and Minerva then woke Annabelle and tiptoed into her mother's room to make sure her morning chocolate had been brought up and that the fire had been lit.

She was about to wake her mother when, to her surprise, the vicar walked into his wife's bedroom, looking about himself with a vague air of surprise as if he had never seen it before.

He had, in fact, hardly set foot in it since his wife's last pregnancy some eight and a half years ago. When Mrs. Armitage had been delivered of twin boys, therefore presenting the vicar with double heirs instead of another girl, he decided, as he privately put it, "to stop the breeding" and thankfully relapsed into a semi-celibate life, only occasionally indulging his lusts, usually around harvest time, with some country girl who was willing and able.

He put his finger to his lips, and signalled to Minerva not to wake Mrs. Armitage but to follow him from the room instead.

He silently led the way downstairs to the parlour. "I'm going into Hopeminster today. There's a horse fair on, and I want you to come with me."

"Alas, I cannot, Papa," said Minerva with sweet patience. "I have my rounds to make and this is the day I read to Lady Wentwater." Lady Wentwater was an elderly widow who lived some two miles beyond the village.

"Well, you ain't," said the vicar. "You're coming along o' me. Annabelle can read to her."

"Why, Papa? You know enough about horses. There is nothing I can tell you on that subject. Furthermore, a horse fair is no fit place for a l . . ."

"Tish, girl. Will you do as you are told! You may browse about the shops until I have completed my business and then we shall have a dinner at the Cock and Feathers before returning home. If you must know why, it's time you spent more time around the men. Get some practice, see? Last Hunt Ball, what did you do? You set yourself up to be chaperone to Annabelle because Mrs. Armitage was sick, and sat there with the dowagers for most of the evening. Now, no more argyfying. Go and tell Bella she's to read, and make the calls, and kiss your Mama goodbye. And find a pretty bonnet!"

Minerva bowed her head and marched upstairs to her mother's room, seething with irritation. She had successfully coped with the boredom of country life by making herself useful and, particularly after last night's shock, she had been looking forward to settling into her usual duties. Now this! The proposed outing to Hopeminster was making her apprehensive, but she mistook her apprehension for nervous boredom, and blamed her father accordingly.

Her mother was awake and sipping her chocolate when Minerva gently opened the door.

"Good morning, darling," said Mrs. Armitage in a faint voice, holding up a faded cheek to be kissed. "I was reading a fascinating volume . . . there it is . . . give it me . . . I shall . . ."

"Mama! Papa insists that I go to the horse fair with him. It means I will not be able to make my calls although he has said Annabelle may do them. But I do not wish to go and . . ."

"You must do what Papa thinks best," said Mrs. Armitage. "Besides, I need new ribbons for my cap. Now, only attend! For you must learn ways to enhance your beauty, you know."

Mrs. Armitage opened the book and fumbled among the lace on her bosom for her quizzing glass. She began to read, peering through the quizzing glass with one eye and screwing up the other into a horrible wink in an effort to see.

"This is called *The Toilet of Flora* and it is translated from the French. Now! You might care to experiment with this "curious varnish" for the face. It says you prepare it by leaving an ounce of gum sandrach and one and a half ounces of benzoin to dissolve in three-quarters of a pint of brandy. It says it gives the skin the finest lustre imaginable! And here . . ."

"Mama! I do not think it necessary that . . ."

"And do you think you can find a green pineapple? It says here that the juice from green pineapples takes away wrinkles and gives the complexion an air of youth! It also says if you can't find green pineapples, onion juice will do—but I declare onion juice is hardly an attractive scent and it does cling so. Do you not 'member when Annabelle had the earache, and we put a roasted onion in her ear, and how she had the smell of that onion on her for at least a week? Yes, you must definitely go to Hopeminster. 'Tis quite providential. Apart from the ribbons, lilac silk, my dear, I need spirits of lavender and some pomatum and, oh, don't forget the pineapple, though where you will get such a rare thing I do not know. Oh, and bring me alkanet root, for I have a mind to make some rouge for you.''

''Mama!''

''Do run along Minerva, I feel quite weak. One of my Spasms is coming on, and I must rest and be quiet.''

Mrs. Armitage sank back against the pillows and closed her eyes.

Minerva gave a little sigh. Mama's Spasms were her ultimate weapon. It would be useless to look for help. She must simply make up her mind to go to the horse fair.

Annabelle was furious and had to be bribed with promises of sugar plums and a novel from the circulating library. Normally, Minerva would not allow a novel houseroom, but Annabelle's temper tantrums were quite formidable. The vicar always threatened to take the birch to her, and Minerva feared that he might very well, and so she spoiled Annabelle unnecessarily, thinking she was protecting the girl from a beating.

Then Minerva was sent back upstairs to change because the vicar took exception to her bonnet, castigating it as dowdy and saying he would not be seen driving a Friday-faced quiz, daughter or no.

At last, they were seated in his racing curricle behind two spanking bays and bowling at an alarming pace along the Hopeminster Road.

Chapter Three

"Osbadiston is selling off his stable," said the vicar, tooling his curricle through the traffic in the main street of Hopeminster.

"Oh, I see," said Minerva, hanging onto her bonnet. And it certainly accounted for the unusual appearance put forward by this normally quiet market town in the middle of winter.

The Earl of Osbadiston was famous for his horses. He was also famous for his gambling debts and so it had transpired he had to sell the one to pay the other. Eccentric as ever, the Earl had opted to put his cattle up for sale at the local horse fair instead of Tattersall's. The vicar alone did not consider the Earl foolish. Members of the Quality who had driven all the way from London were likely to be more in a frame of mind to bid high to justify the long journey than they would be in the comfort of Tattersall's.

And so the sale explained the presence of many dazzling members of the Quality to be seen in the town, both male and female, looking as exotic as birds of paradise. Minerva's eyes grew rounder and rounder.

"Papa!" she cried. "Did you see that lady? She was

wearing practically nothing but thin muslin and gauze. And in this weather!''

"Don't gawk," retorted her worldly-wise father. "They'll take you for a yokel."

"But anyone would stare," protested Minerva. "Look at that little man over there. He's *green!* I mean every single thing he's got on is *green!*"

"That'll be Cope," said the vicar, without bothering to look round. "Wonder what he's doing here. He not only wears green, his rooms are green, his furniture is green, everything's green. Know what they say about him?

" 'Green garters, green hose, and, deny it who can, the brains, too, are green, of this green little man!' He's a Dandy."

"Oh." Minerva digested this. "But he's making himself ridiculous," she said at last. "Why does he do it?"

"He's a Dandy, that's why," said the vicar, turning neatly into the crowded yard of the Cock and Feathers. "They're all like that. Do anything to get attention. One of them shot himself t'other day and left a note saying he was 'tired of buttoning and unbuttoning.' But, mark my words, he only did it to get attention. Now do you want tea while I go on to the fair?"

"No, Papa," said Minerva. "I shall look at the shops and buy a few things for Mama and I shall meet you here in time for dinner."

Minerva edged her way along the crowded street, glad that she was wearing her best bonnet, the popular Regency hat of velvet trimmed with sealskin. The high crown was large at the top and a long ostrich plume was fastened at the right side, brought across the crown and dropped over the left ear.

As the latest edition of *La Belle Assemblée* stated, "Everything now takes its name from our beloved Regent." And so Minerva was also wearing the Regency jacket of cloth trimmed with narrow bias folds and edged with sealskin, and long sleeves with epaulets, the epaulets being the distinctive feature of any garment labelled Regency.

She attracted a deal of unwelcome attention from several

obvious Corinthians who were making their way to the horse fair and wished she had brought one of the maids along. There were some ladies promenading with some of the men, but they were so scantily dressed, so rouged, so outrageous, that Minerva could only surmise she was seeing for the first time that mysterious class of women referred to in whispers as Cyprians.

Still, she managed to complete her shopping without being harassed. The gentlemen were not yet too well to go since they did not wish to addle their brains with wine before the bidding, and so they had not yet become obnoxious. Minerva suddenly wondered how her frivolous sister, Annabelle, was faring with Lady Wentwater.

Annabelle pushed open the tall iron gates that led to Lady Wentwater's house and dragged her feet up the drive. She was in the sulks, with all the attendant miseries of having a thoroughly good fit of the sulks with no one about to inflict them on.

Spoilt by her older sister's indulgence, spoilt by parental neglect, Annabelle was a prey to fits of nervous boredom and temper tantrums.

Lady Wentwater was famous for her lack of money and acid tongue. Her large, draughty, dilapidated mansion was covered in so much ivy that it looked like a vast tree house.

The sky was gray and the wind howled mournfully through the skeletal trees in the drive.

Annabelle rang the bell, remembered it did not work, and petulantly kicked at the door with one bronzed half boot.

It was opened by one of Lady Wentwater's ancient footmen who informed Miss that her ladyship was in the back saloon.

Lady Wentwater was a small, dumpy woman, like a lump of dough into which someone had pushed currants for eyes and a piece of cinnamon stick for a mouth. Her clothes were old and musty and smelled of some horrible things, two of which a lady was not supposed to know about.

"Where's Miss Armitage?" she wheezed. The pug on

her lap wheezed as well, the clock on the mantel wheezed prior to striking the hour, and the servant bringing in the tea tray wheezed in reply. It was as if the whole world had become one large all-encompassing bout of asthma.

"Minerva has gone to the horse fair at Hopeminster with Papa," said Annabelle, sitting down dismally beside the tea tray and eyeing the tiny assortment of stale confections on the cake plate.

"Gone to bid for one filly and auction off the other," gasped her ladyship.

"I don't understand."

"You ain't s'posed to. Drink your tea and read. What have you brought?"

"I didn't bring anything," said Annabelle. "I thought you supplied the books."

"Address me as my lady when you speak to me, girl!"

"My lady," said Annabelle through thin lips.

"That's better. Well, since your sister ain't here, you may read this. But don't tell her, mind! She don't like novels and she would preach me to death!"

Somewhat startled to learn that this formidable lady was afraid of her sister, Annabelle drank the tea which she was sure had been brewed from tea dust, returned canisters and impedimenta back to the teapoy, and asked for the book and some extra candles, for the room was growing excessive dim.

After much grumbling, Lady Wentwater agreed to the ordering of candles, insisting cheap tallow ones be brought.

No one had ever found out much about Lady Wentwater, thought Annabelle, as she waited for the candles to be lit. No Wentwater appeared in the peerage, and yet no one had thought to challenge Lady Wentwater or call her an imposter. She dubbed herself a widow, but of the late Lord Wentwater, there was no lingering sign; no portrait or miniature.

A tiny fire crackled on the hearth, warming Lady Wentwater's musty skirts and vanishing in the frigid air before it reached Annabelle. Defiantly Annabelle hitched her own chair nearer the fire and asked whether my lady wished her to begin reading at the beginning of the book. It was Mr. Hugh Walpole's, *The Castle of Otranto.*

"No, girl, begin at the marked page. Page 401."

Annabelle gloomily opened the book. It would have been lovely to begin at the beginning, instead of reading a bit at the end, where one did not know who all these characters were, or what they had been up to.

She began to read in a clear, loud voice, convinced that anyone of Lady Wentwater's age must be deaf.

" *'What! is she dead? cried he, in wild confusion.*

" *'A clap of thunder at that instant shook the castle to its foundations; the earth rocked, and the clank of more than mortal armour was heard behind. Frederic and Jerome thought the last day was at hand. The latter, forcing Theodore along with them, rushed into the court. The moment Theodore appeared, the walls of the castle behind Manfred were thrown down with a mighty force, and the form of Alfonso, dilated to an immense magnitude, appeared in the centre of the ruins.*

" *'Behold in Theodore the true heir of Alfonso! said the vision.*

" *'And having pronounced these words, accompanied by a clap of thunder, it ascended solemnly towards heaven, where the clouds parting asunder, the form of St. Nicholas was seen, and receiving Alfonso's shade, they were soon wrapped from mortal eyes in a blaze of glory.' "*

Snore!

Annabelle looked up and stared in disbelief at Lady Wentwater.

She was asleep.

How on earth could *anyone* fall asleep during such a splendid tale.

Annabelle eyed the book greedily. There would be no harm in taking a quick look at page one. . . .

The early winter's evening settled down over the scrubby estate and the fields outside. Crows winged to the rooky wood, and the shadows thickened in the musty room. The rising wind howled about the eaves.

All of a sudden something made Annabelle lift her eyes from the page. The door handle was slowly turning.

Slowly, with a great creaking of hinges, the heavy mahogany door to the saloon swung open.

A tall, cloaked figure stood on the threshold.

Annabelle's hand flew to her lips and she let out a little gasp of fear. The figure, looming in the shadows, seemed to have walked out of the Gothic tale on her lap.

And then it strode into the candlelight.

It was revealed as no horrible spectre, but as a tall young man with a pleasant open face, a quantity of light brown hair artistically arranged in the Windswept, wrapped in a many-caped Garrick which he swung from his shoulders, revealing an impeccably tailored bottle green coat over buff breeches and glossy hessians. The whiteness of his cravat made Annabelle blink.

He made a magnificent leg. "I am Guy Wentwater, my lady's nephew. Do you exist? Have you a name? Or are you some faery vision?"

Annabelle dimpled prettily and rose and dropped him a low curtsy.

"I am Miss Annabelle Armitage," she said. "I was reading to your aunt but she fell asleep. It's very late. I must leave."

His pale blue eyes mocked her. "So soon? And we so newly acquainted? But you shall not escape me. I am come to stay with my aunt. Since she is asleep, I shall escort you home."

He picked up the book and studied its title with some amusement.

"Particularly as you will no doubt be seeing ghouls and ghosts behind every bush."

"I do not read novels," said Annabelle primly. "I was merely entertaining Lady Wentwater."

"And she so fast asleep? Come along Miss Annabelle. . . ."

Minerva began to wish she had not delayed to study the architecture of Hopeminster church.

The streets were narrow and dark because of the overhanging Tudor buildings and, as she made her way to the inn, although it was only half past three in the afternoon, the day was already dark and the streets were full of noisy and roisterous bloods.

Normally calm and poised in the familiar surroundings of the village of Hopeworth, Minerva became nervous and bewildered in the crowded streets of the county town. Twice she took a wrong turning, twice she had to sidestep a group of noisy men who tried to bar her way.

At last, she recognized the main street and hurried towards the inn.

At the entrance to the courtyard stood an elegant group of three gentlemen and two ladies.

The gentlemen were dressed in the first style of fashion, as were the ladies. They all seemed very tall and grand, and made Minerva feel small and countrified.

She was about to edge past them since they took up most of the entrance to the courtyard, when one of the tallest of the men turned and looked full at her.

For some reason, she felt breathless and flurried and her hands began to shake, and before she knew quite what had happened, she had dropped all her parcels.

Without waiting to see if any of the group were going to help, Minerva stooped to retrieve her possessions.

One of the lady's voices, high and petulant, came to her ears. "If I had a lady's maid as clumsy as that, I would dismiss her on the spot."

As she blushed with humiliation, a mocking masculine voice quite near her ear, said, "Come, Amaryllis. A lady's maid would not sport such a fetching bonnet. Allow me, ma'am."

Half crouched over her parcels, Minerva noticed that the tallest man was also stooping to help her, while his companions looked on.

"There," he said in a languid voice. "I think I have them all, ma'am, apart from those that you have yourself. 'Strordinary, fatiguing sort of business, parcel-collection, heh!"

Minerva straightened up at the same time as the gentleman, and looked up into his face. A pair of cat-like green eyes looked down at her with an unwinking stare. Holding her parcels cradled in one arm, he swept off his curly-

{ 29 }

brimmed beaver with the other and made her a low bow. His hair gleamed in the light of the inn lantern, curled and scented and pomaded. He was wearing a blue swallow-tailed coat with silver buttons over doeskin breeches and glossy black hessian boots with jaunty little tassels. He had a beautifully shaped mouth, too beautiful for a man. His rather heavy lids gave him a slightly dissipated air. The hands, now holding both parcels and hat, were long and very white with polished nails.

His cambric shirt was so fine it was almost transparent, the edge of the frills being rolled and delicately stitched.

There was something awesome about such an amalgam of exquisite tailoring and barbering and manicuring. And to Minerva, something decadent and repellent and, yes, *foreign*.

"I shall see you presently," said this Exquisite to his friends, without once removing his eyes from Minerva's face. "I shall take this lady into the inn and deposit her shopping in some convenient place. Allow me, ma'am."

"Really, Sylvester," came the voice of one of the ladies. "Must you concern yourself with doing the civil to yokels? We should return as soon as possible. I, for one, have no desire to spend the night here."

"Leave me alone, all of you," said Minerva, now thoroughly incensed.

"You heard the lady," said the tall gentleman languidly. "Leave us alone. Now, ma'am, if you will allow me . . ."

He began to walk towards the inn and Minerva had perforce to follow him.

"You shall answer to my father for this insult," she said to his uncaring back.

"Charmed to make his acquaintance, ma'am," was the lazy reply. "I shall perhaps be staying here after all."

Minerva's conscience stabbed her. She had been unfair. This man had not insulted her. His companions had, but that was another matter.

It was her Christian duty to give him a full apology.

Minerva shrank back momentarily at the entrance to the inn. It seemed full of wild drunken masculinity. Her companion patiently held her parcels while she looked in the coffee room, in the tap and in the dining room. Of the vicar, there was no sign.

Her eyes stung with tobacco smoke, her ears were deafened with noise, the low beams of the old inn seemed to press down on her.

"I must find the landlord," she said wildly to her tall companion.

"I shall call him for you," said the Exquisite patiently.

"But you will never be heard above all this hubbub."

"Yes. I think I will."

They were standing in the small entrance hall. The tap was on one side, the coffee room, leading to the dining room, on the other.

The tall gentleman deposited Minerva's parcels on a small table which held a brass jug of wilted flowers, a riding crop, and a beer tankard, and dug a hand into the pocket of his coat—which was, of course, in the pleats of the tails—and drew out a handful of money. Some he threw into the coffee room and some into the tap.

The silence was sudden and immediate. No matter how loud the noise may be, no matter how rowdy the company, no matter how engrossed in conversation, there is nothing that effects a silence so much as the sound of falling money.

"Landlord!" shouted the gentleman, into the hush.

A small, thin, wiry man came bustling up.

"Mr. Boyse!" said Minerva thankfully, to the landlord. "Have you seen Mr. Armitage?"

"I sees vicar a whoiles back, Miss Armitage. He says he's taken a private parlour and he's bespoke two rooms for the night. Seems he's selling an'orse to some gennleman."

"I don't understand," said Minerva, looking bewildered. "He came to buy . . . Oh, very well."

"So if you can find your way, miss. It's upstairs, second door on the roit. Thank 'ee, and I'll tell missus to fetch the tea tray or sumpin'. Dinner'll be soirved as soon as vicar comes."

Minerva marched to the narrow inn stairs and started to

mount. At the third stair, she remembered her parcels, her escort, and that she owed him thanks and an apology.

She turned around. He was standing at the foot of the stairs, holding her parcels, which he had picked up from the table.

Her family would have recognized in Minerva's fixed stare and lofty profile that she was about to make one of "Merva's noble apologies."

"Sir," she said, throwing back her head. "I owe you an apology. I was abrupt with you, forgetting that any insult I may have received in the inn yard did not come from you. I thank you also for your kindness and service to me." She stretched out her arms, rather in the manner of a maiden on a Greek urn to receive her parcels.

She had not realized that changing from the thrown-back attitude to the Greek-goddess-receiving-sheaves-of-corn-stoop was too sudden a switch of posture to make on a steep inn stair, and she tumbled forwards down the stairs on top of him.

He simply subsided gracefully under her weight so that he was lying full length on the inn hall floor with Minerva on top of him while several rowdy bucks and bloods roared and cheered their encouragement, some going so far as to suggest the positions ought to be reversed.

"Unhand me, sir," said Minerva, blushing furiously.

"Damme," complained the tall gentleman, looking up into her eyes. "How can I unhand you when I haven't even got you? It's you, ma'am, who should unhand me. I can't move, you know, with a chest full of lady and my arms full of parcels. Now can I?"

Minerva scrambled to her feet, wishing she were dead. It was all a nightmare. She, the stately organized Minerva to whom the whole Armitage family turned for sage wisdom and advice, to be made to look so ridiculous.

"Papa!" she cried thankfully, seeing the familiar burly figure in the doorway of the inn.

"Sorry I'm late," said her father cheerfully. "Evening Comfrey," he added to Minerva's companion, who had risen to his feet. "I'm fair sharp-set. Let's above for dinner."

And to Minerva's confusion, her father reached a plump arm up to the Exquisite's shoulder and pulled him towards the stairs.

But the tall gentleman disengaged himself, murmured that he would first have to make his apologies to his friends, bowed to Minerva, handed her her parcels, and withdrew, saying he would join them in ten minutes' time.

Minerva could barely contain herself until they were in the private parlour with the door closed behind them.

"Papa! Who *is* that gentleman?"

"Oh, that's Comfrey. Lord Sylvester Comfrey, the Duke of Allsbury's youngest. All the crack, y'know. Rich as Golden Ball and some say he's got more social power than Brummell."

"If that is the sort of man with whom I am to consort when I make my come-out in London, then I would rather not go," said Minerva, removing her bonnet.

"Well, see here," said the vicar sternly. "I ain't forcing you to marry him this evening. I'm trying to sell him one of the bays he's got his eye on. Says there was nothing at the fair to match it, and there wasn't. He'll pay a good price, so I don't want any of your missish airs. If you don't like him, keep quiet. He can do you a power of damage in London if he takes you in dislike."

"I do not like Dandies," said Minerva in a low voice.

"Here! He ain't a Dandy, and don't you go a-calling him one, see? He's an out and outer. Apart from Alvaney, I wouldn't give any of them Dandies house room."

"Surely Mama will be worried if we do not return home?"

"No, she won't, 'cos I sent a boy to the vicarage for our clothes. We're staying here tonight and that's that. I can smell snow, but let's hope it holds off until tomorrow. Shhhh! I hear a step on the stairs."

The door opened and Lord Sylvester stood surveying the vicar and his daughter through his quizzing glass. Then he let it fall and walked lazily into the room.

Minerva could not understand why she disliked this man so much, but dislike him she did.

Nonetheless, she managed to present a pretty picture during dinner, while the two men discussed horseflesh and blood-lines. She had glanced in the looking-glass before sitting down and knew she was looking her best. The cold of the afternoon had brought the roses to her cheeks and her black hair gleamed with health. But not once did Lord Sylvester glance in her direction and after some time Minerva began to feel unaccountably piqued.

And yet she sensed his brain seeking out her own. She sensed he was observing her somehow, although he did not look in her direction. She put this fancy down to the fact that the wine was heavy and fortified with brandy, and to the heat of the room. But as the meal went on, she began to feel increasingly nervous, so that when he at last addressed her, she dropped her fork with a clatter on her plate.

"I believe we are to have the pleasure of seeing you in London next Season, Miss Armitage?"

"Yes, my lord."

"And are you looking forward to all the balls and parties?"

Minerva was overcome by a childish desire to appear different; to make an impression. In short, to show off.

"No, my lord," she said. "I would I could stay at home, caring for my brothers and sisters and attending to the wants of our parishioners. It is by helping others that we gain pleasure for ourselves."

"Indeed! Then why plunge into the fleshpots of London with such gay abandon?"

"I must," said Minerva, half shutting her eyes . . . another irritating mannerism. "My family demands it of me."

"Why?"

Minerva met her father's fulminating glare and blushed. She could not possibly explain that she had to catch a rich husband to save the Armitage fortunes.

She bit her lip and said nothing.

"I mean," pursued that infuriating voice, "one would think you were being forced to go. Is that the case?"

"There must be some way of breeding in cry without breeding anything out," said the vicar, ruthlessly changing the subject. "Mostyn's hounds are quite remarkable for their muteness. But Beaufort's pack would give you palpitations of the heart—the best pack in England after Belvoir.''

Lord Sylvester picked up the conversational lead and turned to hunting. Soon there was nothing for Minerva to do but retire to her room and leave the gentlemen to their port.

"Your traps are in room six," said her father. "I shall be in room two if you need anything. We shall not stay late. I am tired and I am sure his lordship is as well.''

Minerva kissed him on the cheek, curtsied to Lord Sylvester, who bowed in return and then held the door open for her.

"Good night, Miss Armitage," he said softly.

Minerva's gray eyes flew up to his face. His green eyes watched her with that steady gaze, and despite herself, her eyes fell to the beautiful curve of that sculptured mouth, before she muttered a hasty "good night" in reply.

Once she reached her room, she knew sleep would not come. The elegance of Lord Sylvester and his friends had made London seem like a formidable place. Who were those haughty ladies who had been with him? Was he attached to either? Was he married? Oh, what did it matter! For the sake of her brothers and sisters, she must train her mind constantly to higher thought.

She drew out a small leather bound volume called *Meditations on the Destiny of the Soul* and proceeded to read, sitting in a battered armchair in front of the dying fire.

Try as she would, she could not concentrate. It was not that Lord Sylvester had disturbed her in any way, she told herself firmly. The horrendous noise from the tap below was enough to wake the dead.

The next thing she knew, the steeple clock was chiming two in the morning. She had fallen asleep.

Minerva felt stiff with cold. She threw a shovelful of coal on the embers of the fire, and opened up the battered trunk to lay out her nightclothes.

A crumpled gray flannel shirt, a Kilmarnock nightcap, and a roll of gentleman's small clothes met her startled gaze.

Then she realized with some irritation that the inn servant had given her her father's trunk by mistake and had no doubt given her father her own.

She felt tired and gritty from having slept in her clothes and, after some hesitation, decided to find her father's room and exchange luggage, wondering all the same why her father had not discovered the mistake himself.

Picking his trunk up in one hand and the bed candle in its flat stick in the other, she pushed open the door, searching along the narrow inn corridor for room two. The room numbers were scrawled in lead pencil on the whitewashed walls of the corridor beside each door.

After bumping the trunk up several stairs and down several stairs, she found room two and tried the handle. The door swung open.

"Papa!" whispered Minerva, advancing towards the bed and holding the candle high. The bed was empty.

She lit a branch of candles on the mantelshelf with the bed candle and, in the sudden blaze, saw her own trunk standing by the bed.

Where could the vicar be?

The curtains were not quite drawn.

Minerva went to the window, opened it, and looked out into the inn yard which was brightly lit by moonlight.

As she watched, two figures appeared under the light of the lamp which hung over the arch leading into the courtyard of the inn.

One was her father, the other that of a woman. Her father said something and the woman's loud coarse laugh rang out on the night air. Then the vicar stooped and gave his companion a hearty kiss and a slap on the bottom.

He shouted good night and walked towards the inn.

Minerva drew back from the window.

Now she knew why her father had so mysteriously managed to book two rooms and a private parlour on the day of the horse fair, seemingly at the last moment. He had, in fact, booked them well in advance. The whole expedition had been planned to look like a sudden impulse. Taking his eldest daughter had been camouflage. He had had an appointment with a lady of the town.

Minerva knew that her father was sometimes unfaithful to her mother. Men were like that. But never before had she seen an actual demonstration of the fact.

She felt lost and bewildered and hurt. She also did not want to see her father when he returned to his room.

Grabbing her own trunk, she blew out the candles on the mantel, picked up her bed candle, and hurried back along the way she had come. She thought she would never find her room again, when suddenly she saw a bumpy six on the whitewash and, with a sigh of relief, pushed open the door, and walked in.

Her nerves were by now quite overset. She gave herself only a perfunctory wash, noticing that the cans were only half full and that the towels were damp, and resolved to complain to the landlord about this sloppiness in the morning. The room appeared larger than she remembered and smelled slightly of brandy. Furthermore the bed curtains were drawn and she was sure she had left them drawn back.

She changed into her nightgown, brushed out her hair, and tied a pretty lace nightcap on her head.

Minerva turned and faced the bed.

Sanctuary!

To plunge down on that feather mattress and pull the covers over her head and sleep the trials and tribulations of the world away!

As she had done when she was a little girl and frightened of the dark, Minerva blew out the candle, made a rush for the bed, and dived headlong through the bed curtains.

"Oooof!"

The breath seemed driven out of her body as, for the second time since she had come to Hopeminster, she landed flat on a masculine chest.

"Manna from heaven," murmured an amused voice. Before she had time to recover her wits, one firm hand pressed down on her back, one other firm hand forced up her chin, and a hard mouth covered her own.

She jerked her mouth away and opened it to scream but she was neatly rolled over onto her back and the full weight of a man's body pinned her to the bed, and that seeking, demanding mouth found her own.

Far back in Minerva's throat came a choked little sound of pure fright.

Immediately her lips were freed, and the heavy body rolled off her.

"Don't scream," came a languid drawl that Minerva now recognized as that of Lord Sylvester. "Let me light the candle and see who I have in my bed."

A little yellow flame sprang up, a hand pulled the bed curtain further back, and Lord Sylvester's handsome face looked into Minerva's frightened one.

"How dare you, my lord," said Minerva, recovering her courage, and realizing she had only to scream to bring her father and the inn full of servants. "How *dare* you lurk in my room!"

He leaned back against the pillows and clasped his hands behind his head. "On the contrary, Miss Armitage, this is *my* room."

Minerva shut her eyes tightly and then slowly opened them hoping that there was some mistake. But his lordship was right. It was undoubtedly his room. Now that she looked clearly, it was indeed larger, and the furnishings were slightly different.

In alarm, she hopped from the bed and walked around to stand, shivering, on his side. In a halting voice, she explained about the trunks, and about how she was sure it had said "six" on the wall.

He lay, propped up on the pillows, quite at his ease, his nightcap at a rakish angle on his head, and his face looking almost translucent against the white lace of his nightshirt.

"There's no need to keep clutching at yourself like that, ma'am," said his lordship. "That thing you're wearing conceals your figure, shape and form to perfection." He raised his quizzing glass. Dear God, the man slept with it! "In fact," he went on, "it's flannel, I would say. Keep the winter chills out."

He smiled at the trembling Minerva in a comforting sort of way and half closed his eyes.

There was one thing about Minerva. She knew where her duty lay and she would perform it no matter what the cost.

Aware that he was speaking the truth and that her nightdress was more concealing than any ballgown, she dropped her arms to her side, threw back her head, half closed her eyes, and declaimed, "I am willing to marry you, sir."

His lordship's eyes flew open. Then they half closed again like the eyes of a drowsy cat. "Getting deaf," he murmured. "I could have sworn you said you were going to marry me."

"But I did!"

"Why? Not, why did you say it, but why do you want to marry me?"

"It is my duty."

"In what way?" said Lord Sylvester, wriggling his broad shoulders slightly against the pillows to make himself more comfortable.

"Because I have compromised you."

"Dear me. You know, Miss Armitage, you wouldn't keep falling down on things and people if you tried keeping your eyes open and looking straight in front of you. That's better. Now, the gentleman, may I remind you, is usually the one who is considered to have compromised the lady, for the simple reason that loss of virginity in a man is a duty not a disaster. 'Get rid of it,' my father said to me when I was only sixteen and hardly knew I had got it, if you take my meaning. Extraordinary when you come to think of it . . . education." Lord Sylvester yawned delicately and stretched, his unwinking green eyes now wide open and fixed on Minerva's face. "You've got to learn to shoot well, hunt well, and drive to an inch, not to mention fencing and dancing.

"And then when you've mastered all that, they start pestering you to lose your virginity. You have no idea how lucky you are to be a lady, Miss Armitage. So you see you cannot possibly have compromised me."

"I was trying to be polite," said Minerva in a stifled voice. "The fact is, sir, I agree with you. I am the one who has been compromised."

"Not unless someone saw you visiting my room. Did they?"

"No, my lord."

"Well, there you are. Nothing to worry about." Again he stretched and his heavy eyelids began to fall.

Minerva watched him in furious silence.

"You are surely not going to sleep?"

"Why not?" he mumbled. "It's my bed and my room and my fatigue. Of course, if you would like me to kiss you again, I shall wake up like a shot."

"I most certainly do not!"

"Then there you are," he mumbled. "Good night."

"You might at least help me with my trunk," said Minerva, picking it up and walking to the door.

"If I helped you with your trunk, we might be seen together, tramping around the corridor of this inn in our nightrail. And I really don't want to get married, you know. I have managed this three and thirty years quite comfortably without it."

"No one asked you, my lord," snapped Minerva.

"Dear me. And I thought I had just received a proposal."

"Ooooooh!"

Minerva marched out and stopped herself from violently slamming the door behind just at the last minute.

The wavering, treacherous candle now revealed that the room she had just quit was indeed number nine. Number six was located after much searching and Minerva was finally able to settle down to sleep.

It was a silent journey back to the vicarage in the morning. A fine powdery snow was beginning to fall and the journey took longer with only one horse to pull the vicar's curricle.

Try as she would, Minerva could not quite banish the irritating Lord Sylvester from her mind. She had hoped to see him before they left in the morning so that she could treat him with all the contempt he deserved, but of his lazy lordship there was no sign.

At last she asked her father if he had enjoyed a good night's sleep.

"Excellent," said the vicar without a blush. "Always sleep better away from home."

Minerva had not the courage to tell him that she had found

him out. Would her husband become like that once they were married? Were all men like that? Would Lord Sylvester . . . ? Oh, forget the man!

An excited Annabelle was awaiting them when they arrived, bursting with news. She could hardly wait until Minerva had delivered the packages to Mrs. Armitage, before dragging her off to their bedroom to pour out the news of Lady Wentwater's handsome nephew.

"And he is to leave next week because he has business in Bristol," gasped Annabelle, hopping with excitement. "Mama met him and is quite *épris*. She was doubtful at first since it appeared he was in *trade*. But it seems he is in collecting of some sort and has many ships. Black ivory! That's what he collects. In Africa! Is it not exciting?"

Minerva listened patiently to the outpourings, frowned slightly when she learned Lady Wentwater had given her sister a novel to read, promised to smile on Mr. Wentwater when he came to call. All the while her busy mind was wondering whether Annabelle might be the one, after all, to save the family fortunes, thereby saving her, Minerva, from going to London.

At last Annabelle demanded news of Hopeminster and her eyes grew rounder when Minerva said that they had taken dinner with Lord Sylvester Comfrey and that Papa had sold him one of the bays.

"Even *I* know of Lord Sylvester," said Annabelle. "Josephine and Emily saw him when they were last in London and could talk of nothing else. He is accounted very handsome."

"He is a fop," said Minerva coldly. "He cares nothing for anything or anyone. He is engrossed entirely in his own foppery."

"Oh," said Annabelle, disappointed. "And he did not pay you any particular attention?"

Minerva dropped her eyes. She did not wish to lie. Then she realized Lord Sylvester had been obliged to pay her attention simply because she had entered his room by mistake.

"No," she said. "And I am glad of it."

Her conscience gave a nasty little twinge but for once Minerva firmly ignored it.

"Tell me more about Mr. Wentwater," she said.

And Annabelle needed no second bidding.

Chapter Four

Mr. Wentwater came to call quite often and put the Armitage family in a fever of hope and excitement. His carriage and horses were of the first stare, his clothes denoted the rich young man. Even Mrs. Armitage roused herself from her sick bed to take over the reins of the household and to take Annabelle into Hopeminster to buy her jaconet muslin for a new gown.

Minerva would have liked to press Lady Wentwater for a few more details about her nephew, but Annabelle became quite hysterical when Minerva offered to continue the reading to Lady Wentwater, not wishing to lose a minute of Guy Wentwater's company.

The vicar pronounced him a fine young man and, after a successful day's hunting in his company, declared him to be an excellent fellow, an out-and-outer, with a beautiful seat on a horse.

Minerva could not help contrasting Mr. Wentwater's easy and open manners with the studied, aloof elegance of Lord Sylvester and almost envied her sister her good fortune in finding such an eligible suitor without having to go through any of the agonies of a Season.

At last, as the term of his stay with his aunt drew to a

close, the vicar formally invited him for dinner, and the vicarage was thrown into an uproar for quite two days before. The odd-man, Harry Tring, had put on weight and his butler's livery had to be let out, John Summer, coachman, groom, kennel master and whipper-in had the duties of footman added to his list and one of father's old plush game coats had to be refurbished with gold braid, his bald head had to be covered with the vicar's second-best wig, Minerva had to lend him a pair of her best flesh-coloured stockings since the footman's stockings would show and hers would not.

Mr. Wentwater was expected to propose that very evening and the family were warned to give Annabelle and Mr. Wentwater every opportunity of conversation together.

The couple were placed next each other at dinner and it was soon to be seen they were quite eager with each other. Minerva watched Guy's handsome face and the way his pale blue eyes lit up when they rested on Annabelle's face and admitted to a pang of pure jealousy.

But at least it seemed as if she would no longer have to go to London.

Her father had called her into his study that afternoon. "See here, Minerva," he had said. "It looks as if this Wentwater is going to pop the question. He has led me to believe he has quite a fortune in his ivory business. It's no use me asking that old woman, Lady Wentwater. She won't tell anyone a thing. But it means if Annabelle is first to go, there will be no need for you to go to London. I ain't a greedy man and one fortune in the family is enough. We can wait until the other girls grow up if you want to stay here."

Minerva found herself a prey to mixed feelings. She would have sworn a minute ago that the whole idea of London was repugnant to her, but now, now that it seemed to be sliding away, she felt a recurrence of that old, stifling boredom.

"It's a pity Comfrey didn't take a fancy to you," sighed the vicar. "But that would be flying too high."

"Perhaps his affections were otherwise engaged," ventured Minerva. "When I first saw him he was with two other gentlemen and two exceedingly elegant ladies. Perhaps one of them . . . ?''

''Oh, *them*,'' said the vicar. ''Amaryllis Wadham and Jennie Delisle—two of the highest-flyers in Town. *Very* expensive.''

''You mean . . . ?''

''Yes. But I shouldn't be talking to you about it. Ladies like you shouldn't know that women like that exist.''

''But they were so grand, so haughty, so well-dressed!''

''Your Duchesses don't come any grander than a high-class Cyprian,'' said the vicar sourly. ''I should know, I . . .

''Here! Off with you. Those type o' lightskirts'll ruin a man more than gambling or drink. 'Which hast devoured thy living with harlots.' Luke, chapter thirteen, verse thirty. So there!''

Now Minerva, watching the happy couple across the table, could not help wondering why she did not feel relieved that her proposed Season in London was being put aside. She was now free to devote herself to good works and the welfare of her family.

Well, she may as well start by paying attention to the conversation.

''This mining business of yours in Africa,'' the vicar was saying. ''I believe you told Annabelle it was to do with ivory.''

''Black ivory, Mr. Armitage,'' said Guy Wentwater, toying with the stem of his wineglass, his eyes veiled in a secret smile.

The vicar's face turned quite purple and for one awful moment Minerva thought he was going to have an apoplexy.

Then he went white as he had been puce a moment before and said in measured tones, ''I do not like your trade, sir!''

Mr. Wentwater gave an infinitesimal shrug as if he had heard it all before.

Daphne, the thirteen year old of the Armitage brood who had startled her family by putting her hair up and assuming the airs of a dowager, said primly, ''I do not see what is the matter, Papa. We have to have black ivory or how else would we have black keys on the pianoforte?''

"Silence!" roared the vicar. "Mr. Wentwater means slaves. The trade in black ivory is the trade in human souls and human bodies. So many Jimmys to be branded and flogged out in the West Indies."

Mr. Wentwater raised a lace handkerchief to his lips to hide a smile. It was perhaps to be expected that the vicar as a member of the Church of England should feel obliged to put on some sort of show, but he felt sure his family would not share his views.

He was unfortunate, however, in that the Armitages took a highly personal view of the whole of the slave trade.

The Earl of Osbadiston had a black butler called Jimmy whom the Armitages all knew and met on their infrequent visits. Jimmy was a sort of god to the young Armitages. He could make catapults, manufacture dolls out of practically nothing, and even counsel Mrs. Armitage wisely on her various imagined ailments. Added to that, a year before the Abolition of the Slave Trade in 1807 the Armitage family had travelled to Bristol to stay with a richer branch of the family, their mother's cousin. They had heard horrible tales of death and suffering among the negroes who were transported across the world, packed worse than cattle.

And so they were unusual in condemning a trade that most English people were unaware of, or, if they knew about it, did not care either way the slightest.

The vicar was a simple countryman and not a very good prelate. But he was loyal to his friends and had taken an immense liking to the Osbadiston butler. And so for him, the slave traders were sending so many wise and wonderful Jimmys away from their native land to serfdom in the Indies.

To Guy Wentwater, it seemed as if one minute he was the adored centre of attention, and the next, left in a cold, isolated place on the other side of a vast gulf where the Armitage family huddled together, looking at him with accusing eyes. Although the slave trade was officially abolished, it was well-known that many adventurers such as Wentwater continued to supply slaves to America and the West Indies and no one thought the worse of them for it, apart from a few cantankerous reformers.

"I must plead my case, I see," he said with a light laugh.

"I would like to talk about something else," said the vicar, and proceeded to give a very long and boring dissertation on hunting which took the party through the meal to the port and walnuts stage, when the vicar terminated his lecture by saying he was too fatigued to stay awake a minute longer and it was "high time the children were abed."

The evening abruptly broke up with embarrassment on the side of the Armitages and growing fury on the side of Guy Wentwater.

He was allowed no time alone with the fair Annabelle and, in fact, she was the first to quit the room.

By the time he had reached his aunt's mansion, Guy Wentwater's anger had purged all softer feelings for Annabelle Armitage from his mind.

He had made a mistake, that was all. He should never have bestowed his distinguished attention on a member of a lowly and queerly religious country family.

As for Annabelle? Minerva sadly pushed open the door of the bedroom, expecting to find that young lady in tears.

But Annabelle was brushing her hair as usual, all unconcern.

"I'm sorry, Bella," said Minerva softly. "I hope it is not too great a blow."

"Pooh!" said Annabelle carelessly. "I am relieved. It was as good an excuse as any. He frightened me. His caresses were becoming too intimate."

"Annabelle!" shrieked Minerva. "He never . . . ?"

"No, he never. Just kisses and things. But he did pant a bit, Merva," giggled Annabelle. "Do you think all men are like that?"

"I do not know," said Minerva primly. "Say your prayers, Annabelle, and pray let us forget about Mr. Wentwater."

"Oh, Merva, you are so *prim!* Don't look so cross. It was fun for a while. I felt quite the heroine when I thought I would be saving the family. But, ah me! a slave trader, of all disgusting things." She giggled again. "He looked quite taken aback. You must admit, Merva, it does come as rather a surprise when Papa turns out to have principles! He is the most unusual clergyman, and really only quotes his Bible when he can't think of anything else to say.''

'' 'Honour thy father and thy mother.' Remember the fifth commandment,'' said Minerva severely.

"Oh, you're just as bad," laughed Annabelle. "One of these days that prim façade of yours is going to crack, Minerva, and then what a shock you will give us all. Ah, well, it seems you must go to London after all!''

"So I must," said Minerva, looking startled. Then she wondered why the idea of a London Season, which had filled her with dread such a short time ago, should now produce such a pleasurable mixture of anticipation and elation.

In the short winter days and long winter nights that followed, Minerva found to her horror that the image of Lord Sylvester became stronger rather than fading. She was tormented with dreams from which she awoke with the pressure of his lips still on her mouth.

Before, she had enjoyed a fairly comfortable conscience. Sin was something to be combatted in everyone else, not in her own chaste bosom.

She could not confide in Annabelle for fear of sullying that young lady's pure mind. Minerva would have been alarmed had she guessed how sullied Annabelle's mind really was. Annabelle's remarks about Mr. Wentwater's intimate caresses, Minerva had firmly decided, were mere imagination. Perhaps Mr. Wentwater had forgot himself so far as to press Annabelle's hand more warmly than he should, but no gentleman would go further.

Her conscience told her to excuse Lord Sylvester for kissing her, for she had literally thrown herself at his head.

At last, unable to bear her evil thoughts any further, she decided to confess all to her father.

The vicar was at first too taken aback at the idea of his daughter having visited his room in the small hours and finding him absent to pay much attention to what she was saying.

When he finally grasped that she had leapt into Lord Sylvester's bed, he gazed at his blushing and trembling daughter in amazement and asked her brutally if his lordship had "got his leg over."

"Over what, Papa?" was Minerva's answer.

"Look here," said the sweating vicar. "Begin at the beginning and tell me all he did. Think of me as your confessor rather than your father."

And so in a halting voice, with many stops and starts, Minerva told of that kiss and the subsequent conversation.

The vicar's high colour slowly ebbed. "By Jove, Comfrey's a gentleman!" he exclaimed. "Such restraint! Such thoughtfulness! But if he didn't do anything and he ain't going to *say* anything, what ails you, Minerva?"

Minerva hung her head, her black glossy curls hiding her face.

"I have lustful dreams, Papa," she whispered.

The vicar's face brightened. "Do you, b'Jove?" he said, cheerfully, rubbing his hands. He had long thought his eldest daughter a cold fish and was beginning to despair of her "taking" during her forthcoming Season. But she was his daughter and he knew she would never forgive him if he tried to reassure her. If Comfrey had sparked those feelings in her, it augured well for the success of her London debut. On the other hand, although it was good to know these very human feelings were there, one could not risk encouraging them in case the girl did anything silly.

"I am afraid those feelings must be purged, Minerva," he said severely. "Much as it goes against me to punish you, I think you will realize I am only doing it for your own good. Now, those hounds of mine are growing fat and lazy on account o' all the frost and they sore need exercise. John Summer has enough to do. So you go along to the kennels, and take the fattest and laziest out for a walk. Tell John, Warrior, Wonder and Rambler are most needy. Take them as far as Highcap Hill and back. You won't have time for any thoughts but sleep after that."

Highcap Hill was a good ten miles away across country.

He never expected Minerva to actually walk twenty miles, but he had not allowed for the streak of martyrdom in his daughter. Minerva felt the punishment did indeed fit the crime and she was too exhausted even to eat by the time she arrived back home.

The vicar decided to keep her at it. He did not want Minerva getting frisky in the springtime and running off with some unsuitable farmer. Better to keep her cold till he got her to London. Then her blood could run as high as it liked.

He had worries enough himself. The Bishop of Berham had been making rumbling noises, indicating he thought the vicar of St. Charles and St. Jude spent too much time on the hunting field.

If only the American colonies had not separated from Britain, thought the vicar sourly. Virginia would have been the place to go. Evidently the revolution had rather spoiled things there. In the old days, when the vicar was a boy and Virginia was British, that colony abounded with hunting parsons who went at their pursuits energetically. "The race must end in a dinner, and the dinner must end under the table."

The vicar admired General Washington, not as a military leader, but as a huntsman. Up until 1774, Washington had spent most of his time on the hunting field, often with his wife, Martha, riding at his side, and Thomas Jefferson "as eager after the fox as Washington himself." He had built his kennels a hundred yards from the family vault, simply because that location had a good spring of running water.

The vicar's meditation on past glories was interrupted by the arrival of the post boy, bearing a crested letter, affixed with a heavy seal.

It was from Lady Godolphin, saying she would be delighted to bring out Minerva provided the girl married well enough to reimburse her ladyship all expenses accruing therefrom.

So that was one thing settled, thought the vicar with a sigh. There was nothing else he could do but stave off his creditors and hope for a happy outcome.

Meanwhile Minerva plodded the long miles across country in all weathers, the hounds at her heels. The gruelling exercise had the desired effect. By the end of the day, she was too tired to even remember what Lord Sylvester looked like. The news of Lady Godolphin's invitation left her indifferent.

It was only at the end of March that the Reverend Charles Armitage, preaching his daughter's sermon from the pulpit, realized that daffodils were blowing among the tussocky grass around the gravestones and that his eldest daughter's face was unfashionably windblown.

In a bare two weeks time, Minerva must leave for London.

At dinner, he berated his wife for having neglected the girl's appearance with the result that Mama had one of her Spasms and took to her bed.

All at once, Minerva was thrown into a fever of anxiety. The long, hard exercise which had drugged her mind was stopped. Old fashion magazines were studied and hands raised in despair over the expense of the toilettes portrayed therein.

How the hours flew, the days flew. One minute London and its Season and its fashionable world seemed such a long way away, and the next, it was rushing upon her, hurtling towards her in clouds of bonnets and gloves and stockings and cosmetics and fans and reticules.

Lady Godolphin had promised to furnish a wardrobe, and Minerva's detailed measurements had been sent to London. But she would need to *arrive* looking bang up to the nines. How the Armitage girls stitched and sewed! Even lazy Annabelle did her best. She had grown very quiet since the departure of Mr. Wentwater, and Minerva often wondered uneasily whether Annabelle ever thought of him.

Their cousins, Josephine and Emily, were to be in London as well, and tormented the vicarage girls by dropping in at all hours, arrayed in quite delicious gowns.

As the hour for departure approached, Minerva became ill with apprehension and misery. She felt very young and defenceless. She was being torn away from everything that gave her life purpose and meaning and maturity. Here at home, she was virtually head of the Armitage household. In London, she would be just another hopeful debutante.

If only women did not have to marry!

But there was nothing else for a well-brought-up girl to do except to find a husband. Minerva, although she could supervise and choose a menu, had never been taught to cook. She knew nothing about politics and was only vaguely conscious of the war that was raging in the Peninsula. She spoke indifferent French and worse Italian, played the piano competently and sang rather well.

She knew that when she arrived in London life would be centred around men. She knew that if a girl danced prettily, had good manners, listened well and had a talent for "making the agreeable," then she should be able to secure a husband.

But there was no one she could really consult about the sudden return of those embarrassing emotions. Emotions were things we all suffered from, inflicted on us since the Fall, but not to be encouraged or indulged. Any excess of emotion was vulgar in the extreme.

Her face had become tanned with all the exposure to wind and weather, and Josephine and Emily reported to Lady Edwin with great glee that "dear Minerva had sadly gone off in looks."

Spring had crept across the Berham countryside. Great fleecy clouds trailed their shadows over the greening fields. The crimson catkins of the black poplar swung in the wind, violets and primroses and snowdrops starred the grassy banks beside the Hopeminster Road.

And then two days before Minerva was due to leave for London, a violent snowstorm swept in from the East, plunging the members of the vicarage into despair. Mrs. Armitage, who had grown quite animated over all the feminine preparations, promptly took to her bed, school was cancelled, and nervous tempers ran high. The vicar was locked in his study, trying to compose his sermon, longing to ask Minerva to write it for him, and then deciding he had better get used to doing it himself.

But the very next day, a thaw set in. Pale yellow sunlight flooded the countryside, and once again birds sang among the delicate green tracery of the spring leaves.

The vicar's travelling carriage had been revarnished and the rents in the upholstery repaired. John Summer was to act as coachman and the odd-man as groom. Betty, the housemaid, had been bought a new print gown and told she was to travel as far as London with Miss Armitage and return with the carriage.

The vicar emerged from his study to ask Minerva if she

would like to "say-goodbye" to the dogs she had exercised, and was mortally offended when she said she had no affection for them at all.

Like many country squires, the vicar was inordinately proud of his personal hunt, and loved all his hounds as if they were family pets. He muttered that Minerva had something up with her brain box but did not press the matter.

Minerva resented the hunt, the hunters, the hounds, and the whole horrendous expense that went on keeping them. She was now thoroughly frightened of the unknown London that lay waiting for her, and felt that Papa might have made shift to retrench, instead of putting her on the marriage market as if he were leading a bull to the fair at Hopeminster.

The county of Berham lay comfortably close to London and the journey could be accomplished in two days, in easy stages.

All at once it was the morning of Minerva's departure.

The day was perfect, a sky of egg-shell blue stretched overhead, unbroken by a single cloud.

Minerva was wearing a plain cambric morning dress, made high in the neck and with a short train, and let in around the bottom with two rows of worked trimming. Over it, she wore a pelisse of green sarsnet trimmed round with a narrow fancy trimming and pinned with a gold brooch. On her head, she sported a Lavinia unbleached chip hat, tied down with a broad white sarsnet ribbon, and she wore a small white cap underneath with an artificial rose pinned on the front. A plaid parasol, York tan gloves and green silk sandals completed the outfit.

Even Annabelle was taken aback by the transformation of her elder sister. "Oh, do marry someone rich, and *soon,* Merva," she begged, "so that I may have pretty gowns as well."

The boys reminded Minerva that their future schooling lay in her hands, Mrs. Armitage had a long list of patent medicines as a farewell present, and the remaining four little girls clung pathetically to her skirts and cried their eyes out.

Lady Wentwater had sent around a copy of Mr. Porteous's sermons with a sour inscription on the fly-leaf saying she would not be needing it any more and had had enough of "improving" books.

Josephine and Emily, who were not to leave for London until the following week, arrived to say goodbye, and with many glances and titters tried to convey to Minerva that she looked the veriest dowd, but their jealousy was fortunately plain enough to be quite heart-warming.

And then Minerva was in the carriage with the sunlight glinting bravely on the new coat of varnish and the final hen feather plucked from the squabs. Betty, the housemaid, was crimson with excitement, and the other servants began to wonder if the mistress's Spasms were infectious.

John Summer cracked his whip. The two plough horses strained at the traces.

And they were off!

Minerva felt a lump rising in her throat as the little party on the steps of the vicarage grew smaller and smaller and then was suddenly lost to view as the heavy coach rumbled around a bend in the road.

The gold thatch of the cottages clustered around the village green shone like new-minted guineas. Ducks bobbed on the silky waters of the village pond. A swan sailed majestically across, leaving a broad V in its wake. Smoke climbed up from chimneys. The squat majesty of St. Charles and St. Jude began to recede. A crowd of locals outside the Six Jolly Beggarmen sent up a rusty cheer.

Past the ornamental gates of the Hall rumbled the ancient Armitage coach, over the hump-backed bridge which spanned the River Blyne, around past the weedy estate of Lady Wentwater with primroses peeping from cracks in the mossy walls. A sharp right turn at the gibbet, and out onto the drying mud of the Hopeminster Road.

Soon dust began to rise from the road, so Minerva put the glasses up, and sat very straight, frightened to lean back in case she crushed her bonnet.

After some time, the town of Hopeminster came into view.

The sun was blotted out as the coach trundled under the overhanging eaves of the Tudor buildings.

Past the Cock and Feathers. Minerva's heart gave a painful lurch. A tall man in curly brimmed beaver and blue coat was standing at the entrance to the inn courtyard. As the coach passed, he turned, as if aware of her gaze. He had a thin foxy face and pale eyes.

But memories of Lord Sylvester came rushing back. Minerva decided that Lord Sylvester must be a sort of devil to conjure up such sinful feelings in her breast. She took out her Bible and began to read, her eyes wandering among the begats until she fell asleep.

Chapter Five

Lady Godolphin lived in great style in Hanover Square. At first Minerva had been startled at the expensive address, thinking that her patroness rented a floor from another family. She had naturally assumed that anyone who was in need to be paid back for the expense of a Season must surely be in difficult circumstances.

But it appeared that the whole vast residence was the property of Lady Godolphin.

They had broken their journey at a posting house on the outskirts of the city and Minerva had insisted that they start as early as six, fondly imagining everyone in London kept country hours.

An imposing butler informed Miss Armitage in hushed tones that my lady was yet abed and not likely to quit it until noon, and had left strict orders she was not to be disturbed.

A stern housekeeper showed her to a pretty suite of rooms on the second floor.

"It's like Kensington Palace," breathed Betty the maid, looking about her in awe.

"You may start unpacking my trunks," said Minerva

rather severely to cover up for the fact that she was as awed as the maid.

The sitting room was decorated in Nile green and gold and contained some very fine pieces of furniture. A William and Mary chest of drawers in oyster veneer stood against one wall, and a Louis XVI writing table at the other. There were portraits by Zoffany, Reynolds and Lely.

The bedroom boasted a modern shell-shaped bed which had been designed to go with a set of shell-shaped chairs from the last century. The bed looked decadent to Minerva's prim eye, with its supports of mermaids and dolphins and its total absence of canopy and curtains. There was a painting by one of the Italian masters above the bed, *Presentation of the Virgin*, with everyone concerned wearing very blue robes and very gold halos.

Fine oriental rugs covered the floor and heavy damask curtains of green and gold hung at the windows which overlooked the square.

There was a powder closet and a dressing room off the bedroom. Minerva realized she was looking at all this magnificence with her mouth open, and set herself to help the maid unpack.

There was a great noise and shouting below the windows. She crossed the room and looked out. A noisy party of bloods were roistering their way around the square, faces swollen and flushed with wine.

Minerva drew back quickly. By the end of the Season would she be married to one of *them?*

She resumed her unpacking and was grateful for the arrival of a tea tray.

When the pretty gilt clock on the mantel chimed one o'clock, Minerva was wondering whether she should venture out into the streets. It did not look as if she would ever see her hostess. The carriage and Betty were to start the long journey back to Hopeworth as soon as possible, but she felt timid, and did not want to send the maid, her last link with home, away.

At last, a gigantic footman in green and gold livery scratched at the door and informed her that Lady Godolphin was awake and anxious to see Miss Armitage.

Minerva felt at liberty to dismiss her maid and a very tearful farewell she made of it. She pressed a guinea into Betty's hand, thereby depleting her pin money by a tenth, and then followed the stately footman down the stairs to a suite of rooms on the first floor.

Already in her mind, she pictured Lady Godolphin as a stern aristocrat, and all Minerva hoped was that she could curtsy low enough without disgracing herself by falling on the floor.

Lady Godolphin was seated by the fire in her sitting room when Minerva was ushered in.

She was like none of the pictures that Minerva had conjured up in her mind.

Lady Godolphin must have been, at least, in her late fifties. She was round-shouldered and had a heavy bulldog face. She had small, pale-blue eyes under wrinkled lids, and her sparse grey hair was covered by an enormous turban of ruby velvet.

Her morning gown of velvet was cut very low, exposing a generous, if flabby bosom. Her muscular arms were very freckled. Her figure was tough and stocky. In fact, in shape, she was surprisingly like the vicar. But it was not that which shocked Minerva. It was the fact that my lady was thickly painted. Her face and bosom were covered in white enamel and her cheeks were brightly rouged. Her large mouth was painted crimson, and her stubby eyelashes were covered in a thick coating of lamp black. When she moved, long ripples of old flesh strained under the confines of the paint on her bosom making her look like a badly stretched canvas.

And worst of all, she had a moustache, bristling with white paint, above her upper lip.

She bounced to her feet at Minerva's entrance and rushed to kiss her, and Minerva contrived not to recoil before the barrage of peculiar scents that assailed her nostrils, from lead paint to a perfume called "Miss In Her Teens," brandy, rose water, and sour sweat.

"Faith, but you are pretty enough to turn heads, Miss Armitage. I had not much hope of any beauties coming out of the Armitage stable though your Mama was quite a belle in

{ 58 }

her youth," said Lady Godolphin with a surprisingly charming girlish laugh.

"We shall be the *succès fou* of the Season. For I tell you I am wearied of the single state and mean to find a husband for myself. The first of your gowns should arrive this afternoon, and Monsieur Lognon himself is to give you a delicious coiffure. We are to the Aubryns this evening. They are monstrous fashionable and although 'tis not yet the Season, we can study the market, for everyone who is anyone goes."

"This evening?" whispered Minerva. In Hopeworth, anyone who had made a journey even to Hopeminster was expected to rest for a day after at least.

"Yes, is it not exciting? Now, how old would you say I was?"

"I do not know," said Minerva tactfully.

"No," crowed Lady Godolphin. "For you expected to find an old quiz and not a young matron like myself. My hair is grey, 'tis the only disadvantage, but that shall be changed this very afternoon. How is your papa?"

"Very well, I thank you, my lady, and sends his . . ."

"And the gown you are to wear to the ball is *ravissante*," said Lady Godolphin, who rarely listened to a word anyone else said.

"I had not thought to go out this evening," ventured Minerva. "I am a trifle fatigued . . ."

"But your hair is not fashionable. All off! It must all come off!"

"I do not believe in improving overmuch on what the good Lord has seen fit to give me," said Minerva primly.

This time Lady Godolphin heard her and looked at her in some dismay. Then she brightened. "Well, I suppose you can be trusted not to prose on like that in the ballroom."

As the day hurtled past in a welter of fittings and pinnings and parcels and hair clipping, Minerva began to feel sure she had been sent to London for some Divine purpose. It was obvious Lady Godolphin was a brand to be saved from the burning. It was disgraceful that a woman of her years should consider herself a young miss, should paint like a Cyprian, and talk like a groom. For as the agitation of preparation went on, Lady Godolphin's speech became as broad as the language of the hunting field, and was saved from ultimate coarseness by her lack of education and frequent malapropisms.

"Follicles!" was her favorite oath, having once heard it uttered in a whisper by a hairdresser and having immediately taken it to mean a part of the anatomy that had nothing to do with the roots of the hair.

Minerva folded her lips in an even tighter line. She would endure this ball and do her best to please. But her purpose was surely to bring some virtue into Lady Godolphin's frivolous mind.

Having found someone she thought needed her, Minerva rapidly began to recover her poise and submitted to all the dressing and preparation with good grace. She had feared that the ball gown Lady Godolphin had chosen for her would be scandalous, but Lady Godolphin was no fool, and had no intention of puffing off a virgin by making her look like Haymarket ware.

Her gown was a gossamer satin robe of celestial blue with a demi-train; stripes of white lace had been let into the cross way of the skirt which had a broad lace Vandyke pattern around the bottom. The short sleeves were fastened up the front by a row of pearls. Her hair was arranged *à la Greque* in soft curls next to the face, and her head-dress was composed of braids of hair threaded with pearls and cornelians. White kid gloves, carefully wrinkled to cover very little of the arm below, a long tippet of swansdown, and pearl earrings completed the ensemble.

Lord and Lady Aubryns had a town house in Grosvenor Square which was within walking distance. But fashion decreed they must arrive by carriage and be delivered at the door, and so they had to wait nearly a whole hour in the press of traffic before they were deposited outside the Aubryns' mansion.

Lady Godolphin was wearing a thin, white muslin gown which had been damped to reveal every swelling bulge of her stocky body. On top of her newly flaxened hair, she wore zebra feathers, which, combined with her bright paint, made her look like a primitive native on the warpath. She contented herself while they waited in the line outside the Aubryns by shouting abuse at various other coaches. "Give way!" she screamed, thrusting her feathered head out of the carriage window.

"Call yourselves coachmen? Well, you ain't. Follicles, the lot of you. Great bunch of follicles!"

Minerva's eyes began to glow. Lady Godolphin was a marvellous sinner, a splendid sinful soul crying out to be saved. Her excitement at the prospect of reforming Lady Godolphin brought delicate pink to her cheeks and a luminous shine to her large eyes. She knew that Lady Godolphin would be stared at and giggled about and be a general object of scorn. For who could look at Lady Godolphin without experiencing pity or contempt?

But it was Minerva who winced before the battery of eyes when she entered the ballroom. The first set of country dances was over, and the pairs of dancers were promenading around the floor, before the next dance. To Minerva it seemed as if hard assessing eyes were staring at her from every corner of the ballroom. No one made the pretense of looking at her sideways or behind fans. Some gentlemen produced quizzing glasses, levelled them in her direction, and raked her boldly from head to foot.

No one seemed to pay the slightest attention to Lady Godolphin.

Minerva was introduced by her companion to various hard faces and hard eyes and then they made their way to a line of gilt rout chairs against the wall.

"All the world and his wife is here," said Lady Godolphin, fanning herself vigorously. "I shall point them out. There is Lord Alvaney. Oh, and there is Mr. Brummell. Lady Sefton is yonder talking to Mr. Cope, the little man in green. Someone will ask you to dance soon, I am quite sure. Are your garters tied tight?"

"Yes," said Minerva tersely. "But not too tight," she added in a whisper. "It is not good to constrict the circulation of the blood."

"Fiddle," said Lady Godolphin. "Garters not tied tight

is the most treacherous of things, I remember . . . ah, here, if I am not mistaken is your first cavalier. Mr. Jeremy Bryce, handsome, spendthrift, a rattle.''

Mr. Bryce was a tall young man with a formidable pair of cavalry whiskers. His face seemed to be a little bit to one side; his nose bent a little to the right, his eyes were focussed a little to the right, and his mouth was twisted up on the right. He had very long legs encased in extremely close-fitting black tights, and during the dance, these legs seemed to be everywhere, waving about in the air like those of an injured insect.

There was not much chance for conversation until the set was over and he and Minerva promenaded around the ball-room.

''You are newly come to town, I believe,'' he said. ''What do you think of the Season?''

''I do not know,'' answered Minerva, who had made up her mind to be honest at all costs. ''The Season has not begun.''

''Oh, you know what I mean,'' he said, a shade of irritation creeping into his voice. ''The Season is like *this.*''

Minerva studied the ballroom, the richly dressed figures, heard the occasional snatch of malicious gossip, saw the anxious eyes of the debutantes.

''I think it is all a farce,'' she said in melodious tones. ''I think society cares too much for worldly things and too little for their immortal souls.''

''Really, ma'am. I see Lady Godolphin is anxious to speak to you and so . . .''

He promptly deposited her beside Lady Godolphin—who had not been looking for Minerva at all—and walked off, mopping his brow.

''I hope you didn't waste any time dallying with young Bryce,'' said Lady Godolphin. ''Absolutely no money there.''

Before Minerva could reply, her next cavalier came up. ''Widower, fancies young gels, comfortable income, nothing exceptional,'' came the words of her chaperone, just before her new partner bowed over her hand. He was introduced as Harry Blenkinsop. Again the dance—which was a country one and lasted quite half an hour—afforded little opportunity for dalliance or conversation.

But once again, as Minerva walked around on the arm of her partner, as was the custom, her eyes searched the ballroom, disliking what she saw, not admitting for one moment it was because the tall figure of Lord Sylvester was not present.

"I was staying once with the Osbadistons," said Mr. Blenkinsop, "and had the honour of hunting with your father's pack. What an experience, Miss Armitage! He has that pack so drafted for speed and bottom that when they are running should one dog lose the scent, another is at hand immediately to cover it. They are so close and so ready, you could cover the whole pack with a blanket! How proud you must be of your father!"

"My father is a man of the cloth," said Minerva quietly. "I am proud of the fact that he has given up his life to the service of the church."

"But, dash it all, the man has bred the best hounds outside Belvoir . . ."

"At great and unnecessary expense," said Minerva firmly. "It seems a great deal of time and organization and money to kill one animal."

Mr. Blenkinsop stopped stock still, and glared at his fair partner, who, until a moment ago, he had been considering the prettiest girl in London. "You would have us *shoot* the fox?" he demanded harshly.

"Shoot it, strangle it, poison it . . . it's surely all the same," said Minerva, aware that she was behaving very badly indeed and not caring one whit. She was being *honest*, and she was not letting the foibles and fribbles and falsities of the Season impinge on her soul, and that was a very heady feeling indeed.

If Minerva had giggled or lisped all these inanities, thought Mr. Blenkinsop furiously, then he could have forgiven her. But her very air of smug superiority was maddening in the extreme.

"Your servant, ma'am," he said abruptly. And turning on his heel, he marched off and left her to find her own way back to Lady Godolphin.

Thanks to the fury of Mr. Bryce and Mr. Blenkinsop, Minerva's fame was spread rapidly through the ballroom, and, for the next two dances, she was obliged to wait, partnerless, beside Lady Godolphin. Lady Godolphin introduced Minerva to several of the other debutantes, good-naturedly hoping to find Minerva a few friends. But Minerva treated her peers to that same brand of righteous superiority that she had inflicted on her partners and she was soon left alone. Completely alone. For an elderly gentleman solicited Lady Godolphin's hand for the dance, and for the first time in her life Minerva knew what it was to be a wallflower. It was then she noticed that Lord Sylvester Comfrey had entered the ballroom. She looked down at the toes of her celestial blue slippers in sudden mortification.

She would hardly admit to herself that she was sure that, when she saw him again, she would be surrounded by admirers, not sitting alone, abandoned even by her chaperone.

She had forgotten how handsome he was. The beautiful tailored simplicity of his evening dress made the other men around him look either overdressed or shabby.

Like Brummell, he was wearing a blue evening coat and white waistcoat, but instead of the tight-fitting pantaloons sported by the famous Beau, Lord Sylvester was wearing light brown kerseymore breeches, with strings to the knees, white silk stockings and shoes with buckles.

As Minerva watched under her lashes, she saw Lord Sylvester being buttonholed by Mr. Bryce. Lord Sylvester raised his quizzing glass and looked in Minerva's direction. Then he dropped it, disengaged himself from Mr. Bryce, and a moment later could be seen talking to Lady Aubryns.

Minerva sat and wrestled with a suddenly overactive conscience. She had been right, had she not, to speak the truth so plain?

"Vanity," whispered her conscience. "You are uncomfortable and feel inadequate so you are using honesty as a weapon to make others feel uncomfortable."

But that could not be right. She had been feeling elated and righteous only a moment before.

Minerva was so lost in the examining of her conscience

that at first she did not quite take in the fact that Lord Sylvester was standing in front of her, looking amused.

"I shall repeat my offer, Miss Armitage," he said. "May I have the honour of the next dance?"

Minerva collected her scattered wits. "Certainly, my lord," she said as calmly as she could, and then blushing furiously as she remembered the feel of his lips pressing down on her own.

"Since we have a few moments before it begins, may I sit beside you?" And without waiting for permission, he took the chair next to her.

He had one hand resting on his knee. That hand which had pressed her down so firmly . . . Minerva blushed again.

"I would ask you what you think of London, but if rumour has it aright, I fear you would subject me to a long and painful lecture on the vanities of society."

"You are impolite, sir," said Minerva. "I fear that some unkind people have found fault with my honesty."

"It appears your honesty has been undiplomatic to say the least. Do you *always* tell the truth?"

"Always."

"Then I am curious to know why my presence makes you blush, Miss Armitage?"

"My lord, the nature of our last meeting was such . . . was to say the least . . . I have very painful memories of our last meeting."

"I remember being very gentlemanly indeed. What exactly distresses your memory so much?"

"I should not need to remind you. You should not ask!"

Minerva sat bolt upright. Two spots of angry colour burned on her cheeks.

"For a young lady who prides herself on her honesty, I find you singularly reticent. I held you and kissed you because I thought a willing young woman had leapt into my bed. Imagine my blushes, my confusion, when I found it was the good vicar's daughter."

"You are mocking me! You were not in the slightest put out. In fact, you nearly went to sleep."

"I always feel sleepy after any great emotional crisis."

"If you choose to mock me . . ."

"Ah, you cannot recognize honesty in anyone else. I am simply telling the truth. Our dance, I think, Miss Armitage."

Minerva could only be glad it was a Scotch reel, and that they were constantly being separated by the figures of the dance.

It was when she was performing the figure eight that she began to feel a sinister slackness about her knees.

Now Lady Godolphin's warning about tightening her garters no longer seemed frivolous.

A look of strain began to appear on Minerva's beautiful features.

She could *sense* the treacherous garters untying themselves.

She stole a quick look down. Her stockings were descending in fat folds about her ankles. Little beads of perspiration appeared on her forehead.

The dance, she knew, would last for quite half an hour. How long had they been dancing? Minutes? Eons?

All the canons of polite society shrieked against her confiding such a disgrace to her partner. She performed an elegant *pas de bas* and sent up a silent prayer.

The garters had been knitted for her by one of the Hopeworth parishioners in a repellent grey wool. Minerva had not thought twice about wearing them. After all, who was going to see her garters?

Now, she decided, they were just about to be exposed to the interested gaze of London society.

To her infinite relief, the dance finished and she sank into a low curtsy in front of her partner. As she did so, she felt her garters slip and fall; a sudden looseness, a sensation of falling silk.

She could not rise.

She *dare* not.

The unwavering green eyes looked steadily down into her own. Was it her imagination? Or did a little spark of mischief lurk somewhere in their depths.

"The supper dance, Miss Armitage," he said.

Still crouched in a curtsy, Minerva looked up at him with wide anguished eyes.

He remained bowed over her, his hand on his heart, waiting for her to arise.

Suddenly he smiled. "You should have told me your ankle was sprained," he said. "It often happens on these slippery floors. If you will but allow me . . ."

He stooped and picked her up. The repellent garters fell to the floor, and, holding her tightly against his chest, he stooped again like lightning and scooped them up.

"Excuse me. Twisted ankle, you know," he murmured as he made his way through the guests, carrying Minerva. "Ah, Lady Aubryns. Perhaps you could show me to some room where Miss Armitage may be able to rest for a little? Miss Armitage has wrenched her ankle."

"Perhaps Miss Armitage suffers from too much rigidity," said Lady Aubryns nastily. She had already heard of Minerva's moralizing.

She was a plump, plain woman with two plump, plain daughters and so she was not overfond of beautiful debutantes in any case.

Lady Aubryns signalled to a footman and murmured instructions.

Lord Sylvester, holding Minerva in what she thought was an unnecessarily tight clasp, strode after the footman, and Minerva soon found herself deposited in a small morning room.

Her rescuer waited until the footman had departed and then dug his hand into his pocket and produced the two limp pieces of grey wool which were Minerva's garters.

Blushing furiously, Minerva snatched them from him and waited for him to leave.

Since he still stood over her as she sat on the sofa where he had placed her, Minerva felt that she must thank him, and did so in an abrupt manner which, even to her own ears, sounded curt and ungracious.

"Say no more about it," said the infuriating lord. "Do you need any help?"

"My lord," said Minerva, with her face flaming. "I appreciate your lying on my behalf. I think, however, I have been embarrassed enough. Please leave while I . . . while I repair the damage.''

"Ah, but we must keep up the fiction, you see. Now if you go behind that screen in the corner, you can spare your blushes. I will then escort you to the supper room where we may enjoy a pleasant conversation.''

"You are most kind, my lord, but again I urge you to leave. You have done enough. Do not think I am ungrateful, but . . .''

"But since you cannot now dance, you would prefer to sit against the wall with the dowagers and wallflowers for the rest of the evening?''

Minerva hung her head. She knew she had made herself very unpopular. It would be agony to sit there, being pitied by all those more fortunate girls. She had been aware of the sharp glances of envy cast in her direction when she had taken the floor with Lord Sylvester, and she was feminine enough to like that.

In all, she felt very confused and very young. At Hopeworth, protected from herself by the needs of others, her parishioners, her family, she really did not have much time for soul-searching. Her brothers and sisters might complain occasionally, but they did not question her sovereignty. As the vicar's daughter, her visits were tolerated by some but welcomed by most, since, to do her justice, Minerva's help was often more practical than spiritual. She read to the sick, looked after children, held sewing classes, and settled disputes.

Her moralizing remarks went unnoticed by people who would have been surprised had the vicar's eldest daughter spoken any other way.

But hard, shiny, frivolous society simply shrugged an indifferent shoulder and damned her as a bore.

For the first time in her life, Minerva began to sense that she was unpopular—and in danger of being considered worse than that—in danger of being considered an Original.

And so she said a meek "thank you" to Lord Sylvester.

Moving in a half crouch, holding her falling stockings in her hands, Minerva scuttled behind the screen and wrenched her stockings savagely back up her legs and lashed them securely with the grey woollen garters.

Then meekly she allowed Lord Sylvester to lead her to the supper room.

She could not help worrying that he would gossip about the disaster of the garters.

"You are not eating," remarked Lord Sylvester.

"I am worried." Minerva's wide grey eyes looked almost black. "I must throw myself on your mercy, sir."

"Really? I find that idea rather exciting. In what respect am I to be merciful?"

"I pray you will not tell anyone about . . . about . . . my accident during the dance."

"My dear Miss Armitage, if I could keep to myself the vastly amusing story of having the vicar's daughter leaping on top of me in bed, I am sure I can keep quiet about her losing her garters."

"Thank you."

"Which is a pity, for Prinny might award me the Order of the Garter if he but heard. Do eat something, Miss Armitage. You are a growing girl."

His mocking eyes rested fleetingly on her bosom, and then returned to her face.

"You must have come as rather a surprise to Lady Godolphin," he went on. "She is rather a scandalous old lady. Godolphin was her third, or hadn't you heard?"

"Her third what?"

"Husband. She has buried three and is said to be on the look-out for number four."

Minerva put down her fork. "That's ridiculous," she said roundly. "Lady Godolphin must be sixty at least. She's very, very old."

"Age does not damp these embarrassing fires that burn within us. . . ."

"I have not the faintest idea to what you are referring."

"To passion, Miss Armitage. Love. Lust, if you will."

"I know nothing about it. Nor do I wish to!"

"So what do you plan to bring to a marriage?"

"You should not be speaking to me like this. No gentleman . . ."

"Should speak so? Look on me as a sort of older brother, Miss Armitage. Unless you become wise to the ways of the world, life with an old rip like Lady Godolphin is going to be full of shocks. I assume you hope to wed this Season?"

"I must."

"Indeed! Why?"

Minerva hesitated. He should not ask so many very personal questions. But he had suggested he adopt the role of brother and that was reassuring and strangely disappointing at the same time. He had no thoughts of marrying her. Nor would he ever have. Minerva certainly never dreamed of marrying the catch of the Season. Perhaps Lord Sylvester would marry eventually, but it would be to some woman of equal rank, fortune and birth.

"My father is in need of money to educate the boys and to . . . to . . . supply us all with the necessities of life. Oh! It all seems so *mercenary*."

"No more so than most of the people in this room," he said gently. "But if you plunge into marriage with a man solely because of his fortune, you are dooming yourself to a life of misery."

"But children," protested Minerva. "I would have children."

"And what about begetting them?"

But he saw from a glance at Minerva's open gaze that she had very little idea of how babies came to be conceived.

"Please let us talk of something else," said Minerva firmly.

"Before we do . . . a word of warning, Miss Armitage. It is a sad life for any woman to be tied to a man that she does not hold in affection at least."

"And how would you know, my lord?"

"Intelligent observation," he said. "I see Lady Godolphin has found a beau."

Minerva turned her head slightly to follow his gaze.

Lady Godolphin was on the other side of the room in animated conversation with a grey-haired military-looking man.

"She has merely found some kind gentleman to keep her company," said Minerva repressively. "Who is he?"

"Colonel Arthur Brian. An old war horse. Married, I'm afraid. No hope of a match there."

"You are funning of course. A lady of Lady Godolphin's age cannot be thinking of anything other than company."

"You must not judge people by yourself," smiled Lord Sylvester. "The Dudleys hold a rout tomorrow. Will you be there?"

"Perhaps," said Minerva, relieved that this blush-making conversation had taken a normal turn. "I do not know yet."

"How many brothers and sisters do you have?" asked Lord Sylvester. "Your good father misunderstood my question when I asked, and promptly supplied me with all the names and pedigrees of his hounds."

Minerva gave a reluctant smile. "That is *very* like Papa. I have five sisters and two brothers."

"What will happen to them if you do not succeed in your objective?"

"I had not thought . . ."

"Do not worry, Miss Armitage. Your face, your figure, and your undoubted beauty are weapons enough . . . provided you do not prose too much."

Minerva took a deep breath. "I appreciate your concern, Lord Sylvester, and I feel sure your remarks are well meant, but they *do* border on the insolent."

"You are right," he said amiably. "What you do or say is no concern of mine."

Minerva should have been relieved. He promptly began to talk lightly of this and that, telling her amusing stories about the entertainments she could expect to enjoy during the Season. But she felt strangely abandoned.

Only a moment before, it had seemed as if the whole magnetism of his personality had been concentrated upon her. But now he had retreated behind a polite façade. No longer was he vibrant, disturbing, upsetting and attractive. He seemed even less than the "brother" he had claimed to be. Minerva finished her meal in the company of a polite stranger.

She kept casting hopeful little glances in the direction of Lady Godolphin. Surely an elderly lady such as she must be wishing for her bed! But Lady Godolphin seemed even fresher than she had been when the evening had begun. Colonel Brian's grey head was bent close to her own and he was whispering something which was making Lady Godolphin's sharp little eyes sparkle.

Ahead lay the terrors of propping up the wall in the ballroom.

Lord Sylvester escorted her back to the ballroom, bowed over her hand and left.

But where Lord Sylvester led, most of fashionable London followed, and Minerva found herself besieged by partners. She could not dance for she had claimed to have wrenched her ankle and so a small court of gentlemen pulled up chairs and surrounded her.

Try as she would, she could not flirt. For too long had she laid down the moral law in Hopeworth. The calm mask of superiority which Minerva used to cover her feelings of inadequacy was quickly put on again. The sight of Lord Sylvester dancing and flirting with a diminutive brunette made her worse. She had been on the point of listening to him, of taking his advice! He was nothing more than a tailor's dummy and he cared for nothing but his clothes.

By the end of the evening, Minerva had become the talk of the ball. The ladies accounted her downright plain. The men called her a moralizing prig. Lady Godolphin heard the gossip and was cross at having to forego a very promising dalliance with the Colonel in order to take her infuriating charge home.

"No, Minerva," she cautioned, while they walked to the carriage. "Not a word until we get home."

Minerva primmed her lips. *She* was not the one who had done wrong! *She* was not the one who had been flirting outrageously!

But when they were ensconced in Lady Godolphin's drawing room and Lady Godolphin started to acidly outline the damage that Minerva had already done to her chances, Minerva began to feel very small indeed.

"I've never heard such a load of follicles in my life,"

raged her ladyship. "Prosing and moralizing like a Methodist! Well, let me tell you my girl, you've got your Pa and the family to think of. And you've got me to reckon with. I ain't sporting the blunt a week longer if you're going to make people feel uncomfortable. Half the eligible young men in London have already taken you in dislike."

"Lord Sylvester did not," flashed Minerva.

"Oh, *him!* He's always doted on eccentrics. Gets his servants off the streets. You've never seen such a rough crew. More like a private army. He's all the crack, I'll grant you that. But even his patronage won't help you for long. If he was serious about you, t'would be a different matter. But folks know that Sylvester has never been serious about any female in his life."

"I really did not say anything very wrong," protested Minerva feebly. "I was only trying to be honest."

"Honest! Some would call it by another name. That silly little flibbertigibbet, Miss Harrison, *would* ask you if you did not think her gown bang up to the mark, and what did you reply? Says you, you think it's very well but the neckline is immodestly low. Now, we all know it was low enough to see her nuptials, but that's neither here nor there, for she went to her friends in tears, and tho' they had been saying just the same thing a bare moment before, they hadn't been saying it to *her*. Now do you see the difference?"

"I felt concerned for her," said Minerva in a low voice. "I only spoke the truth."

"Well, *lie*," howled her ladyship. "One more week, Minerva Armitage. One more week, that's all. And if society has still a disgust of you, back to the country you go!"

Chapter Six

Minerva was determined to try to please Lady Godolphin at the Dudleys' rout. Mr. and Mrs. James Dudley were a fashionable young couple who were determined to remain so, and knew that the road to success was rooms packed to suffocation point.

It took an hour to fight one's way up the narrow staircase of their house in St. James's in order to gasp for air in rooms packed with jostling shoulders and resonant with loud, arrogant voices as the dandy set exercised their wit and presented their *bon mots*. Lady Godolphin spent half an hour talking to Colonel Brian, seemed to remember her charge had yet to be introduced to the host and hostess, performed the ceremony, and then told the bewildered Minerva it was time to go home.

And so they pushed and shoved their way downstairs again and shivered on the doorstep for an hour waiting for their carriage to be brought around.

Minerva had had no chance to be either a success or a failure. Lady Godolphin retired to bed early, and Minerva wrote a bright chatty letter home, saying that everything was wonderful, and privately hoping no gossip of the Aubryns' ball would reach her father's ears. Buried as he was in the country, the vicar seemed able to pick up a surprising fund of rumour and *on dits*.

Annabelle would not have behaved so, thought Minerva. Annabelle would have charmed and flirted. But Annabelle thought a great deal of her looks and already knew to a nicety how to flash killing glances from her blue eyes.

Lord Sylvester had not been at the rout, but two of Minerva's partners of the night before, Mr. Bryce and Mr. Blenkinsop had, and had stared at her very haughtily before turning away.

Well, the sooner they forgot about her the better, thought Minerva before she fell asleep. In fact, they very probably had.

In this, she was very much mistaken. Mr. Jeremy Bryce and Mr. Harry Blenkinsop were at that moment regaling their friends, Lord Chumley and Mr. Silas Dubois, with wildly exaggerated tales of Minerva's moralizing.

"And she's got that nasty way of looking at you as if you'd crept out from under a stone," said Mr. Bryce, crossing his long, thin legs.

The gentlemen had foregathered after the rout in a corner of Hubbold's Coffee House in St. James's. They were all rather foxed and had been working each other up against the fair Minerva for quite half an hour. Mr. Blenkinsop, fat and florid, regaled them with Minerva's view on hunting, Mr. Bryce, his face looking more to one side than ever, told them of Minerva's strictures on the Season.

London had been remarkably thin of gossip of late and so the four gentlemen had had no one to date on whom to vent their spleen. Their malice was bred of boredom. They came to London each year a month before the Season began and, by the time it started, had eaten so much and drunk so much that they were fit to get up to any sort of mischief.

Lord Chumley was fair and foolish with a long lugubrious face and a thatch of tight curly hair. He looked rather like an embittered sheep. Mr. Silas Dubois was all nose. He had very small eyes, a small mouth and a small face which seemed to crouch behind the promontory of his enormous nose. His figure was small and slight. The Dandies cruelly described him as a walking lampoon. But the four gentle-men had one bond in common. Each time one of them looked in his glass he saw an Adonis looking back. All four were extremely vain and fancied themselves as devils with the ladies. They praised each other fulsomely, and this mutual admiration society, together with a deal of strong spirits and fortified wine, did much to keep them separated from reality.

Before this, they had plotted the downfall of some proud society beauty who had snubbed one of them, but all it had ever come to was drinking confusion to the lady. But this evening, the wine was running strong and there seemed to have been something about Minerva which had caught Bryce and Blenkinsop on the raw.

"And she's nothing but a vicar's daughter," drawled Mr. Bryce. "How dare she talk down to me in that deuced prosy way. What she needs is a good tumble with a strong man on top of her. That would soon knock some sense into her head."

"Or into somewhere else," giggled Lord Chumley. "Such a pity one can't do it, though. We could have a mar-vellous bet. I'd give ten thousand to the fellow who could mount her first."

Lord Chumley was the only member of the four who was rich. The other three looked at him in a calculating way.

Mr. Bryce let out a soundless whistle, and then shrugged. "Too dangerous," he said regretfully. "They'd *hang* us."

Silas Dubois leaned forward, his small eyes darting in the shadow of his large nose. "Not if we all stuck together," he said. "Look at it this way. Rumour has it that the Reverend Charles Armitage is hoping his daughter will make a good match and repair the family fortunes. Now, if Chumley here were to court her—he's rich, everyone knows *that*—and we sort of seized our chance when he's got her softened up and then we all stuck together and let her scream and said it was all a hum, well, who's going to believe her? Who'll *want* to believe her? And if one of us does succeed in mounting her, we can then stick together and point out to her that it's in her own interest to keep her mouth shut."

The other three stared at him in speechless admiration.

"But she'll disapprove of us," said Mr. Bryce sourly.

"Not if we play our parts aright," said Silas Dubois. "We'll prose and moralize to beat the band!"

"By George!" exclaimed Mr. Bryce. "You're demned cunning, Silas. Demned cunning."

Silas beamed and his small mouth vanished up under the shadow of his nose.

"When do we start?" asked Mr. Blenkinsop. "And where do we finish? That is, once Chumley gets her on a string, where do we take her?"

"Got an inn out the Barnet Road," announced Mr. Dubois. "Not mine really. Belongs to m'uncle. But it means the landlord will turn a blind eye. Hint at marriage, Chumley, and then say you're taking her to meet your parents. Drop her at the inn and we'll draw straws as to who does the deed."

"One of us or *all* of us," chortled Harry Blenkinsop.

"Fair deal," said Chumley. "That way I can keep my money. I mean, if I'm to organize the whole thing . . ."

The other three looked at him and then at each other. It would spoil the sport if one of them could not gain the prize at the end of it.

"Don't remove the bet, Chumley," said Jeremy Bryce at last. "We'll see you don't do all the work. I have it! We'll give her a chance to go to bed *willingly* with one of us. And whoever she chooses will get the money. If it's Chumley, he keeps it."

This suggestion was hailed with loud cheers, for each of the four privately considered himself irresistible.

They called for more wine, and set themselves to plot and plan.

They were not aware that they already had rivals.

In White's Club in St. James's Street, not so very far away, three gentlemen, who considered themselves leaders of the Dandy set, were discussing Minerva Armitage.

They were Viscount Barding, Sir Peter Yarwood and Mr. Hugh Fresne.

Unlike the previous four conspirators who were all in their late twenties, the three Dandies were in their middle thirties. Both Viscount Barding and Sir Peter Yarwood were married. Mr. Fresne was a bachelor. Lord Barding and Sir Peter kept their respective wives tucked away in the country, preferring to peacock at the Season without the disadvantages of being accompanied by a wife. It also saved money which could be better spent on tailors' bills.

Lord Barding was a plump man with thinning hair. He had a yellowish complexion and a liverish disposition. He was tightly corseted and his shoulders were padded with buckram, making him look even larger than he was. He had very thin legs in tight pantaloons and with his square shoulders and square corseted figure, he looked rather like an animated box.

Sir Peter Yarwood was slim and willowy and drooped. Everything about him seemed to be wilting. Despite assiduous use of the curling tongs, his fair hair drooped in wisps about his ears. His mouth drooped, his eyelids drooped, and his shirt points drooped. He had very long polished nails which seemed to hang at the end of his fingers like icicles from the eaves.

Mr. Hugh Fresne was tall and handsome in what he privately considered a Byronic way and was much given to smouldering eyes and brooding silences. He was always on the point of marriage and for some mysterious reason always backed out at the last moment.

It had quickly become fashionable to detest Minerva Armitage and since there is nothing cosier than a communal resentment, the three dandies found themselves in harmony with each other. Usually, they were ferocious rivals, falling out over the cut of a jacket or the set of a cravat.

All three were very rich, despite Yarwood and Barding's parsimony in leaving their wives at home. They happily spent a great deal of money on themselves and very little on anyone else.

Brummell had remarked languidly that the three gave dandyism a bad name. But they considered themselves the very Pinks of the Ton and dressed in the extremes of fashion in order to attract attention.

After a rubber of whist, they had settled down to tear apart society's latest antidote—the antidote being Minerva

Armitage. No one could quite think in the following weeks who suggested it, but suddenly, after the sixth bottle of port, they had called for the betting book and entered the following bet.

"Mr. F, Sir Y and Lord B do hereby wager 50,000 pounds to be paid to the one who succeeds in winning the *prize* of Miss A's *affections*."

Unlike Mr. Bryce and his friends, they were not planning an assault on Minerva's virginity, but on her dignity. The plan was to get her to fall in love with one of them and then reject her in the most public and humiliating way possible.

And if you wonder if these gentlemen had nothing better to do with their time, the answer is that they had not.

They were absentee landlords, caring neither for tenants nor livestock. They did not belong to the Corinthian set, neither boxed nor fenced nor shot nor hunted. They spent most of the day polishing up their *bon mots* for the evening. The fun was to put some *cove* or *mott* down in order to *put oneself up,* as the latest slang had it. They drank too much, had weak digestions, and hated everybody.

They gambled a great deal and hardly ever won. They dropped names and nicknames of the great and famous, hoping thereby to gain some reflected glory. They heartily despised all military men since any man fighting for his country made them feel obscurely guilty.

Gambling fever gripped the whole of society and the Dandy set in particular. At White's, Boodle's and Brooks's in St. James's Street, it was nothing for a gentleman to lose £30,000 or £40,000 in a single evening. Raggett, the proprietor of White's, used to sit up with the gamblers all through the night, sending his servants to bed, so that he could sweep the carpets himself in the early hours of the morning to retrieve the gold carelessly scattered on the floor.

To practise economy was to be out of fashion, no gentleman would dream of pausing to consider it. They were hell bent on living high in spite of the bailiffs waiting at the door and the *post-obit* bills stuffed out of sight in the ormolu writing-cabinet.

A great deal of time and money also went on clothes and

grooming. Beau Brummell spent some five hours every morning at his toilet. First he bathed in milk, eau de cologne and water, then he spent an hour under the ministrations of his hairdresser whose job it was to tease his thin light brown hair into artistic curls, and then another two hours were spent "creasing down" his starched cravat.

Although the seven gentlemen who were plotting Minerva's downfall hardly represented the Pink of the Ton, they certainly represented all the worst traits of fashionable society.

And so the armies were massing against Minerva who slept peacefully, untroubled by bad dreams or thoughts of her future.

Lady Godolphin had privately vowed to write to the vicar the following morning, asking that gentleman to take Minerva home. It was a pity the girl was such a prude, because she was quite beautiful. But any miss with half Minerva's looks and some town bronze had more hope of succeeding. Lady Godolphin had a soft spot for Charles Armitage, having known him when he was a wild young man. She was anxious to help him so long as it did not mean parting with too much of her own money.

She had spent quite enough already on Minerva's wardrobe and now there seemed little hope that she would ever get any of it back. When she raised her old head from her paint-smeared pillow the following morning, Lady Godolphin began to think about Colonel Brian. Now there was a man! But Minerva would soon find out he was married, if she had not already, and would be bound to spoil sport. By the time her ladyship was dressed and had put a new mask of paint over the old and had donned a new flaxen wig which had arrived only that morning, she was more than ever convinced that she must speed Minerva on her way.

The first inkling she had that life had taken a strange turn was when she found her butler, Mice, in the hall directing footmen to find vases for various pretty bunches of flowers.

"Where did all the buckets come from, Mice?" demanded her ladyship. Correctly interpreting buckets as bouquets, Mice bowed gravely and said they were for Miss Armitage. Miss Armitage was in the Green Saloon, reading the cards.

"Follicles," breathed Lady Godolphin. "She's bin spending good money sending 'em to herself."

Minerva arose at Lady Godolphin's entrance.

She was looking extremely fresh and pretty in a cambric high gown covered with a Spanish robe of pea-green muslin. Her hair was dressed in the "Roman" style, being caught up in a knot on the top of her head with falls of light ringlets.

In her hand were a number of cards. "From your admirers?" said Lady Godolphin in a voice which implied they were no such thing. "Let me see them!"

Minerva handed them over.

Quickly Lady Godolphin flipped through the cards, her eyebrows vanishing under her flaxen wig in surprise. They were obviously genuine.

"God's Hounds!" she said. "Who have we here! Bryce, Blenkinsop, Chumley, Dubois, Barding, Yarwood and the moody Mr. Fresne! Such infusions! Well, well, well. It looks as if you have taken after all. What a set of rattles . . . although Chumley's fortune and Fresne's property are not to be sneezed at.

"Now, what can have brought this about? Twas not your Methodist manners. Ah, I have it! Lord Sylvester Comfrey. *He* sets the fashion."

"I do not wish to seem immodest," said Minerva, "but perhaps I myself may have done a little to attract these . . ."

"Follicles! Mark my words, it's Comfrey. He's always playing tricks. Once he returned from the country wearing his father's old green plush game coat and he needs must go and tell that idiot Chumley that it's all the rage. Chumley tells the whole of St. James's and soon the whole lot of 'em are parading around in the most horrible game coats until they find it's all a hum and Lord Sylvester is his usual tailored self in Bath superfine. Did Comfrey send you flowers?"

Minerva blushed, but said nothing.

{ 81 }

"No. I didn't s'pose so," said Lady Godolphin, answering her own question. "Now, let me consult our appointments. . . ."

Minerva turned away, wishing she did not blush so easily. A bouquet of flowers had arrived, accompanied by an unsigned letter, but she was sure it was from Lord Sylvester. Who else would have sent her such an outrageous poem?

The note hoped that she had recovered from the "rigours of the dance." Then came the poem. It went:

> *"Why blush, dear girl, pray tell me why?*
> *You need not, I can prove it;*
> *For tho' your garter met my eye*
> *My thoughts were far above it."*

On the other hand, he could surely not have meant anything scandalous, thought Minerva as her cheeks cooled. It was perhaps the tone of her own mind that was impure. "My thoughts were far above it" surely meant that his lordship's thoughts were on higher things. Perhaps the high moral tone she had set had influenced his rakish soul. It was *wrong* to think badly of people, Minerva chided herself. He had saved her from a very embarrassing situation and . . . and . . . he had cast himself in the role of brother.

With these comforting thoughts, she was able to turn and face Lady Godolphin calmly.

"We've nothing much here," said her ladyship, thumbing through the card rack, "until this evening. Ball in the garden of the Russian Embassy. Countess Lieven requests."

"Do we have to go?" asked Minerva, rather timidly. She thought nervously of whispers behind hands and staring eyes.

"Go! Of course we have to go. The Countess Lieven is more important than the Prince Regent. Do you know what she says? She says, 'It is not fashionable where I am not,' and that's a pretty accurate summing up of the situation. She's one of the most important leaders of the ton." Lady

Godolphin pronounced ton, not in the French manner, but as if describing a ton of coals.

Lady Godolphin was about to lecture Minerva again on the merits of diplomatic speech when Lord Chumley was announced. Accompanying him were Mr. Bryce, Mr. Blenkinsop and Mr. Dubois.

Minerva threw an anxious look at Lady Godolphin who was grimacing quite horribly and set herself to please. But as Lady Godolphin listened to the gentlemen's conversation, she realized in amazement that they were more moralizing and prosy than Minerva had been. Lord Chumley was bemoaning the evils of gambling, Mr. Silas Dubois was holding forth on the evils of drink, Mr. Blenkinsop became quite impassioned over the fall in church attendance and Mr. Bryce was positively howling for prison reform. Minerva listened quietly but neither agreed nor disagreed.

Lady Godolphin was further startled by the arrival of the Dandy Set in the shapes of Lord Barding, Sir Peter Yarwood and Mr. Hugh Fresne. All at once the Green Saloon seemed to be overflowing with moralizing gentlemen.

Was the girl *never* happy? thought Lady Godolphin crossly. She would have expected Minerva to be in raptures over all this saintly conversation, but Minerva was becoming increasingly distressed and embarrassed.

"Lord Sylvester Comfrey," announced Mice from the door.

Startled faces turned in his lordship's direction.

Lord Sylvester put up his quizzing glass and surveyed the room.

"Now what's *he* up to?" thought Lady Godolphin as Lord Sylvester let his glass fall and walked over and made her an elegant bow.

"I am come to take Miss Armitage driving," he said with a hint of laughter in his voice.

"I say," expostulated Lord Barding, his corsets creaking like the ancient timbers of a prison hulk, "Miss Armitage don't want to go with a rattle like you."

"And how is Lady Barding?" asked Lord Sylvester sweetly. "And all the little Bardings? And Lady Yarwood?" he went on, turning slowly and looking down on the fuming Sir Peter. "Not coming to Town again? Tut, tut! The way you wicked gentlemen keep your wives buried in the country."

Lord Barding and Sir Peter Yarwood scowled by way of reply. They had hoped to charm Minerva before she found out they were wed. Now they were labouring under a heavy handicap. The bet could not stand. They both turned their angry gaze from Lord Sylvester to where their last hope, Mr. Hugh Fresne, sat smouldering Byronically by the fireplace. But Mr. Fresne was convinced that Minerva must be sighing over the romantic picture he presented, and thus he was staring intensely into the fireplace so that he should show his profile to its best advantage.

The rival camp prodded their white hope, Lord Chumley, into action.

"Won't do, Comfrey," he said. "Miss Armitage would prefer to go driving with me. And I'll tell you why. 'Cos Miss Armitage is a high-minded gel, that's why. We was discussing the miseries brought about by gambling 'fore you came in. Now, since you play deep, Comfrey, I feel sure the tone of this conversation would be—"

He trailed off under Lord Sylvester's amazed stare.

Lord Sylvester turned his back on Lord Chumley, affording that gentleman an excellent view of Weston's tailoring at its best.

"Miss Armitage," he said. "I would consider myself the happiest of men if you would honour me with your company."

Lady Godolphin's small, pale blue eyes darted hither and thither, from the self-satisfied look on the faces of Minerva's entourage—for surely she would reject Comfrey—to Minerva herself, who was studying the pattern of the carpet.

Minerva raised her eyes. "I am delighted to accept your kind invitation," she said. There was a sound of several breaths being indrawn in disbelief.

Lady Godolphin's eyes sparkled. Comfrey was simply amusing himself. But she thought that Minerva had made a very clever strategical move.

Some ten minutes later Lord Sylvester picked up the

reins, and his magnificent bays, one of which Minerva recognized as having once belonged to her father, set off at a smart pace.

He looked down at his companion. Minerva's face was shaded by a pretty chip straw bonnet.

"Now why," mused his lordship aloud, "did you decide to favour me with the honour of your company?"

Silence.

"After all, I gather the gentlemen share your views."

"They appeared to do so," said Minerva in a low voice.

"Odso! You shock me profoundly. Can it be that the gentlemen were not sincere?"

"You know they were not."

"Indeed. I thought perhaps you had reformed them."

"I think they are out to make a fool of me."

"You have done that to yourself . . . very ably."

"My lord, you are too harsh," said Minerva furiously "I may have been undiplomatic. But I was merely trying to keep my standards amongst a group of people who appear to have none."

"Highly commendable. But it was perhaps not necessary for you to be so voluble. We do, believe it or not, have some genuine reformers amongst our frivolous ranks. But they confine reforming to the areas in which it will do most good and where their voices will be heard. The House of Commons, for example. They quite rightly use the uncaring members of society merely as a source to raise funds for their projects. Now let us take the sad case of Miss Armitage. You wish to marry well so that you may provide for your family. Charity begins at home. You must keep that in mind. It is a sad fact, but if you wish to entrap a suitor with money, then you will need to be as other debutantes. You will need to flirt, to charm, and above all, to please."

"It is no use now," said Minerva wretchedly. "I am socially ruined."

"Ah, no. If you will enlist my help, I will put it about that you were playing a very great joke. They will never dare admit that they did not see through it. I am powerful enough to bring you into fashion almost by my attention alone. . . ."

"You are arrogant."

"No. I have a great deal of common sense."

"What if I do not wish your attentions?" said Minerva, rather pettishly.

"They should not trouble you in the least since you know them to be helpful rather than serious. Think about it while I go over the characters of your latest courtiers. There is a party of four and a party of three. The four are Bryce, Blenkinsop, Chumley and Dubois. They belong neither to the Dandy Set nor the Corinthians because they affect the worst of the manners of both. They are neither very good, nor very bad . . . with one exception."

"And that is?"

"Mr. Silas Dubois. There are various unsavoury stories attached to his name. Nothing can be proved against him. On the other hand, nothing can be said to his credit, except that he is an expert shot, one of the best in England, I believe. He attaches himself always to a group of weak men and urges them on to folly.

"The party of three aspire to the Dandy Set. That is Barding, Yarwood and Fresne. It was quite amazing to see them present a united front. Usually they quarrel quite dreadfully. Now, I have made you a very civil offer. Have you considered? Do you wish my help?"

Minerva tilted up her head and studied his profile from under the brim of her hat. She felt that his very elegance made him untrustworthy. Even his face had a *manicured* look: the heavy-lidded eyes, the thin straight nose, the beautifully chiselled mouth, the square chin so closely shaved that not a suggestion or shadow of any stubble showed.

His hair was curled and arranged to complement the set of his curly brimmed beaver which he wore at an angle. His shirt points were moderately high, and his cravat was an intricate piece of white sculpture. His long hands holding the reins were encased in fine kid gloves. Life seemed to amuse him. She had a longing to make him angry, to upset him as much as he upset her.

"Do you care deeply for anything?" she asked. "Apart from your clothes, that is?"

One green eye slid round towards her.

"I am sorry if I have offended your sensibilities with my criticism," he said. "Obviously you feel a desire to hit back and any minute now you are going to accuse me of being a Dandy. I see nothing wrong in presenting oneself at one's best. Now, if, for example, I painted my face and wore my hair like the feathers of a Friesland hen, pinched myself in the middle and padded out my chest, smelled like a civet cat, and wore fixed spurs in the drawing room so that I walked like a felon, then I should see room for reform. Now *that* is one way to find if Barding, Yarwood and Fresne are honest in their attentions.

"Tell 'em you can't stand Dandies. You'll have an opportunity tonight. I assume you are going to the Countess Lieven's ball?"

"Yes."

"Then try it. You have begged my question again. Do you wish my help?"

Minerva hesitated. They were turning in at the gates of the Park. Sun slanted in great shafts through the light green of the trees and glinted on varnished panels of carriages, on jewels and painted faces, on glistening horses and silver harness. Fashionables who were not riding walked up and down. A faint haze of dust sent up by the carriage wheels hung in the afternoon air.

Minerva came to a decision. Her family must come first. She must marry and marry well. And so she must repair immediately the damage done to her reputation.

"Yes," she said.

"Splendid," he said lightly.

"Has it not occurred to you that the gentlemen who called on me *might* be in earnest?" asked Minerva.

"No. It had not. But on the other hand, who knows? Your beauty may have reformed them."

Now if you think you do not suffer from any personal vanity whatever—and Minerva was convinced she did not—then it is very hard to recognize the beast when it crops up.

And so, as Minerva became increasingly aware of a few admiring glances cast in her direction, and she turned his last remark over in her mind, she began to chastise herself for having been so hard on the gentlemen who had called on her.

The face that she might have been instrumental in bringing some reform into the decadent souls of at least seven members of society began to take root and flourish.

She would certainly accept Lord Sylvester's offer and try to become fashionable and marry well. But perhaps she could also perform some good service along the way.

Then her conscience gave a nasty twinge. Annabelle would not have concerned herself with moralizing matters like these. Pretty, frivolous Annabelle would have charmed and pleased, and would have been engaged to a rich man before the Season was two weeks old.

Lord Sylvester was giving his full attention to negotiating his team through the press of traffic. Minerva wondered what Annabelle was doing and if she ever heard from Guy Wentwater.

Annabelle Armitage viciously sliced the tops of some thistles by the roadside with a hazel switch, and envied Minerva from the bottom of her heart. While Minerva was driving in Hyde Park, Annabelle was on her way to read to Lady Wentwater.

Lady Wentwater had not mentioned Guy's name for weeks with the result that Annabelle found her thoughts turning in that young man's direction more than she cared. Jimmy, the Osbadiston's butler, had died only the day before. He had died of old age, the doctor had said, much to everyone's surprise, being ignorant of the fact that black does not age so noticeably as white. The much mourned and much loved Jimmy had taken with him to the grave the only black contact in the county of Berham, and with him any immediate human understanding of the horrors of the slave trade.

The attentions of Guy Wentwater seemed more fascinating to Annabelle now that distance lent them a certain enchantment and also because no young man had surfaced to take his place.

Annabelle had found herself becoming increasingly bored and frustrated.

She had avidly read Minerva's letter which had arrived only that morning, but had shrewdly noticed that Minerva had not mentioned the name of one single gentleman.

Probably read them a sermon, thought Annabelle. Minerva's a good sort, but oh, how much better I would do there, and how much better she would do here!

Annabelle had fondly expected her mother to take over some of Minerva's calls, but the very suggestion had brought on one of Mrs. Armitage's famous Spasms.

Minerva had only been gone a few days and already Annabelle was fretting under the weight of the parish chores. Why had Minerva done so *much?* Now all the parishioners expected Annabelle to do the same.

"I am little better than a servant," mourned Annabelle to herself. "Now take Mrs. Jeebles. When she was sick with the ague, Minerva minded her children. Mrs. Jeebles is not sick now but has come to expect the vicarage to supply an unpaid child minder on a daily basis. And if I don't go, and tell Father I have, then Mrs. Jeebles will call at the vicarage, mewing and whining. Perhaps it would all be bearable if Josephine and Emily didn't keep calling to show off their new gowns for London. Both of *them* to have a Season. It's just not fair."

But gradually her anger began to subside. Annabelle's tantrums were always of short duration. It was not long before her usual sunny nature asserted itself.

It was a beautiful late spring day with the spires of the old horse chestnuts shining waxy white in the early evening light. Swallows swooped and dived overhead, and a light haze of fairy green lay over the cornfields, showing where the new crop was already pushing its way up through the brown earth. The air was sweet with hawthorn blossom and damp weedy smells from the ditch beside the road. The evening was golden and very still. A busy duck ploughed across the village pond with her ducklings stretched out in an arrow behind her.

Annabelle stopped on the hump-backed bridge over the River Blyne and threw leaves down into the brown, foaming water, running to the other side of the bridge to watch her small armada sailing underneath.

She was wearing a light blue cambric gown, spotted with dots of darker blue. On her rioting gold curls she wore a little handkerchief, folded, the point towards the back of her head, decorated with artificial cornflowers and blue ribbons. Although this headgear was really fashionable wear for evening, Annabelle had worn it because she knew it to be becoming, and five o'clock was really the beginning of the evening when you thought about it. Her cheeks were rouged by a cosmetic made from her own preparation. Annabelle often made herself a little pin money by selling cosmetics to the women of the village. She had made the rouge from a mixture of 18 parts vermilion, 12 parts tincture of saffron, 30 parts powdered orris root, 120 parts precipitated chalk, 120 parts zinc oxide, 2 parts camphor, 9 parts essence bouquet, 2 parts oil of peppermint and a sufficient quantity of almond oil.

Annabelle had put it on after leaving the vicarage since she kept her cosmetics hidden in a box in the carriage house.

After a while she became tired of throwing leaves over the bridge and set off once again in the direction of Lady Wentwater's mansion.

The trouble with Lady Wentwater, reflected Annabelle gloomily as she settled down in a battered armchair in Lady Wentwater's drawing room, was that she handed over simply splendid novels to be read to her, ones that she had already read most of herself. It was maddening to have to start at the middle or the end. With a little sigh, she began to read:

" 'Prithee,' whispered his Lordship, 'is that queer woman your mother?'

" 'Good Heavens, Sir, what words for such a question! 'No, my Lord.'

" 'Your maiden aunt, then?'

" 'Whoever she is, I wish she would mind her own affairs; I don't know what the devil a woman lives for after thirty; she is only in other folks' way . . .' "

"That's enough," said Lady Wentwater crossly. "That Fanny Burney's so sharp she'll cut herself."

"But it's *funny*," wailed Annabelle, clutching the copy of *Evelina*. "And I have only just begun to read."

"Never mind," said Lady Wentwater in a milder tone. "Guy's back."

"Why?" Annabelle's eyes strayed to the book on her lap. "Is he looking for *white* slaves?"

"Don't be impudent. Why should anyone want a white slave when the British ones only fetch £20 and you can get as much as £144 for a good black."

"British ones?" demanded Annabelle faintly.

"Oh, do you *never* read the newspapers? There were some silly women at Bow Street t'other day. They were offered transportation where they would fetch only a small price each, or they could stay here and be hanged for their crimes. And do you know that one quarter of those silly women chose hanging?"

"Perhaps a quick death was preferable to a slow one on those dreadful ships," said Annabelle with a shudder.

"Well, well, let us not *gloomify* ourselves with such matters. Guy is now a gentleman of great means. He no longer trades."

"How splendid! I hope he sleeps quiet o'nights."

"I thought his trade was the only barrier to your engagement." Lady Wentwater's doughy face was a white blur in the deepening shadows of the room.

"My friendship with Mr. Wentwater is over," said Annabelle firmly. She lit a candle on a table next to her and began to read,

" *'Shall you be at the assembly?'*

" *'I believe not, my Lord.'*

" *'No!—why then how in the world can you contrive to pass your time?'*

" *'In a manner that your Lordship will think very extraordinary,' cried Mrs. Selwyn; 'for the young lady reads.'* "

Lady Wentwater played with the ivory sticks of her fan and studied her young companion's face. Let her read: Guy would contrive to affix her attentions again.

Annabelle at last let herself out of Lady Wentwater's mansion into the cool evening air.

All that was left of the sun was a faint pink line on the horizon.

Sleepy birds chirped drowsily from the ivy which covered the house walls. The warmth had gone from the day and the great iron gates at the end of the short drive felt chilly and damp to the touch.

Annabelle turned over in her mind the intelligence that Guy was back. She reluctantly remembered the feel of his lips against her own. It had seemed so . . . so *sloppy* then. Why should the memory seem so exciting now?

She hurried homewards in the gathering dusk. As she approached the gates of the Hall, she could hear the shrill sound of laughter. Emily and Josephine tried hard to achieve silvery tinkling laughs. They had not yet reached their goal, only managing a sharp-edged sort of titter on a descending scale. Then came the deep sound of a masculine laugh.

Emily and Josephine were talking to a tall, elegant gentleman who had obviously been calling, and was taking his leave.

Guy!

His back was to her. Emily and Josephine affected not to see Annabelle and went on talking feverishly.

But he heard the sound of her light step on the road and turned around.

Annabelle had forgotten until that moment how very handsome he was.

He swept her a low bow.

"I trust you are well, Miss Armitage?"

"Very well, Mr. Wentwater," said Annabelle, dropping him a curtsy.

He gave a little nod and turned back to Emily and Josephine, who flashed Annabelle triumphant looks.

Annabelle flushed faintly, tossed her head and walked off quickly down the road.

So he had lost interest in her!

And he was courting those cats Emily and Josephine.

Well, if his taste ran to silly long-nosed drabs, she wished him well.

But he no longer traded in slaves. And he had looked so

handsome. And she simply could not bear to lose the only beau she had ever had to Emily and Josephine.

She remembered the feel of his hands on her waist. But she should forget him. Once a slave trader, always a slave trader.

But oh! it was so boring in Hopeworth. Why should Minerva have all the fun, flirting and laughing with all those delicious beaux? Annabelle paused, trying hard to imagine her sister flirting and laughing, trying to imagine her being held in a man's arms, and failing completely.

Minerva was, at that very moment, being held tightly in a man's arms.

Lord Sylvester had told his tiger to hold his horses, climbed down and had held up his arms to assist Minerva.

Minerva meant to place her hands lightly on his shoulders so that he could swing her down from the high perch seat of his phaeton.

She was wearing slippers of gold-coloured cloth with bronze tassels, and one of these treacherous tassels caught on a sharp piece of wood under the seat. She stumbled and fell down into his arms, leaving one slipper still wedged in the carriage.

For a brief second she was amazed to discover that a man as cool and elegant as Lord Sylvester could emanate such a *throbbing* feeling, like one of the new steam mechanisms. His whole body seemed to pulse with life and sensuality and masculinity. That beautifully sculptured mouth seemed so very near her own as he held her tightly to his breast. Minerva closed her eyes.

"What a terrible lady you are!" came his cool mocking voice. "Always plunging headlong on top of me."

He swung her to the ground and called on his tiger to retrieve the slipper. He courteously supported her around the waist while she bent and put the shoe on.

Once again, he was mannered and unruffled. Minerva, feeling breathless and shaken, could only think that all the emotion she had imagined coming from him had, in fact, emanated from herself.

"I shall see you tonight," he said, "at the ball."

"Yes. Tonight," said Minerva, turning away.

"Perhaps I shall find myself a wife this Season."

Minerva swung round, eyes wide and startled. Then she dropped her heavy eyelashes to veil her eyes.

"Why not?" she laughed.

He nodded and sprang up into his phaeton and picked up the reins.

Minerva felt depressed and sad. Since Lord Sylvester did not want to marry her, she had not considered that he might want to marry anyone else.

Oh, how terribly tiresome this London Season was!

Chapter Seven

The Countess Lieven was an expert at titillating the jaded appetite of the ton.

Her ball at the Russian Embassy promised to be one of the most exciting events of the year.

In various parts of London, guests who had been honoured with an invitation were fretting over their toilets.

The three Dandies, Barding, Yarwood and Fresne, had gloomily decided that the bet was off, Barding and Yarwood maintaining that their married state was too much of a handicap. But the bet remained in the betting book. Nonetheless, Mr. Hugh Fresne was urged to try to take the field. It was unthinkable that such coxcombs as Bryce and company should succeed.

Bryce and company were faltering in their resolve, since they felt they could not compete against Lord Sylvester. It was left to Mr. Silas Dubois to point out Comfrey's reputation as a rake and his well-known expertise in escaping marriage.

Minerva had managed to throw Lady Godolphin into despair by insisting on reading a chapter of the Bible to that lady while she dressed.

Minerva was merely trying to strengthen her own character before going to the ball where she was determined to flirt and ogle with the best of them. But Lady Godolphin at length cut short the reading by explaining that all those begats made her head ache and brought on a fit of the "vapids."

When they were at last ready to go, Minerva was horrified to find that Lady Godolphin was intending to wear damped transparent muslin, and somehow Lady Godolphin, who had previously considered herself a very strong character indeed, found she had agreed to wear a petticoat under *dry* muslin without quite knowing how Minerva had managed to make her agree to it.

Minerva, she at last decided sourly, was very good at making people feel guilty.

Lady Godolphin had to admit that her charge was in looks. Minerva was wearing a white tunic dress edged with a gold key pattern. Her midnight black curls were caught up on top of her head with a handsome tortoiseshell comb. The wedge heels of her sandals gave her added height. The tan acquired walking her father's hounds had quite faded, leaving her skin delicately tinged with a healthy pink on the cheeks.

Lady Godolphin was looking forward to the ball with all the anticipation of a debutante. Colonel Arthur Brian had promised to be there and had promised to partner her in the waltz, that deliciously naughty dance which had not yet been sanctioned by Almack's.

Lady Godolphin and her charge were forced to leave their carriage some distance from the Russian Embassy as they found their coachman could not make his way any nearer through the tremendous press. Coachmen swore and fought and struck out at each other with their whips.

Minerva was soon to find out the reason for the Countess Lieven's social success. No one else in London could display quite such ingenuity.

The ball was held in the grounds of the Embassy, various marquees and hothouses being used for dancing and refreshments and the inevitable cards.

The walls of the hothouses were tapestried with different coloured moss and the ground was strewn with new-mown grass out of which flowers seemed to grow. Little lamps were placed at the base of each flower stalk, making the blossoms look like jewels. Lamps marked the walks between the hothouses and a clear full moon rode serenely in the sky above, looking almost like an extravagant part of the decoration.

The scented air seemed to throb with excitement. It was an evening made for intrigue, a setting for amorous glances and stolen kisses. It was an evening when it was possible to rid oneself of one's chaperone, for it was quite in order for your gallant to escort you along one of those mysterious walks to provide you with refreshment and to show you the wonders of one of the hothouses.

The air was balmy and warm. Thin muslins fluttered above the illuminated flowers, making Minerva send up a silent prayer of thanks that Lady Godolphin had put on a petticoat, but the clever lighting shining up from underneath revealed that quite a number of the ladies had not.

Lord Sylvester appeared to have worked quickly, for some debutantes giggled and teased Minerva over having made such a game of them all at the Aubryns' ball. The romantic setting was beginning to act on Minerva's senses and, when the dancing started, she could not help watching Lord Sylvester as he danced with a very pretty lady and wishing that he might look in her direction.

Still, he *had* thought of her, and he *had* done his best to restore her reputation, and she must be good and remember the needs of her family. So, aided by the moonlight and the soft air from the pretty gardens, Minerva flirted and laughed and never a serious word did she utter.

It was only when Lord Chumley had danced with her twice and had squeezed her hand too hard and when Mr. Fresne had come to claim *his* second dance, that Minerva remembered what Lord Sylvester had said about the Dandies.

And so when Mr. Fresne with many smouldering glowing looks offered to take her on a tour of the hothouses, she accepted in order to try to find out if these gentlemen were serious in their attentions.

Mr. Fresne looked handsome in a brooding kind of way.

But his evening coat was so padded on the chest and nipped in at the waist that he looked like a pouter pigeon. Moreover, he was wearing fixed spurs which Minerva considered a downright dangerous fashion to adopt for a ball. Also it meant her companion had to adopt a straddling rolling walk, rather like a sailor.

"I do so despise the Dandies, don't you?" she began as her escort led her from the ball out onto one of the pretty walks.

Mr. Fresne, who had just been beginning to think Miss Armitage a very decent sort of girl and not the moralizing prig he had been led to believe, stopped short and looked down at her in astonishment.

"But the Dandies *are* the leaders of Society," he said when he could find his voice.

"Oh, Mr. Brummell is very well," said Minerva. "But it is the ones who wear so much padding and paint that I cannot bear."

Mr. Fresne looked down at the glory of his buckram-wadded chest and felt like strangling her.

After all, a lot of the ladies wore fake bosoms of wax or cotton and one was not allowed to say anything about *that!*

"Of course I do not mean *you,*" went on Minerva, glad that the night was dark enough to hide her blushes. It was so difficult to lie!

Mr. Fresne preened. Of course he should have guessed that, with his manly build, any lady would think his chest was all his own.

"I agree with you, Miss Armitage," he said firmly. "But you must have pity on the fellows who do not have the . . . er . . . build necessary to cut a dash. I say, Miss Armitage, you look deuced pretty in the moonlight."

And she did, thought Mr. Fresne in surprise. All this idea of humiliating her and all that rubbish was unnecessary. He would steal a kiss and carry the tale of it in triumph back to his cronies. Perhaps he might rip a little bit of her dress to show as a souvenir.

But in order to steal a kiss without interference, he would need to lure her away from the lights and into the darkness of the shrubbery. The walks were fairly deserted since at that moment most people seemed to be in the refreshment room or in the ballroom.

"I think we should move on," Minerva was saying.

"Oh, what? Oh, yes, by Jove, quite, quite. I say . . ." He stopped abruptly again, put a hand to his ear, leaned towards the dark shadow of some bushes and said, "Hist!"

"Hist what?" said Minerva, thinking that Mr. Fresne was too stagey for words.

"Oh, list and hist," went on Mr. Fresne. "I hear a little pussy cat in distress."

"I am histing and listing for all I am worth and I do not hear any cat."

"But," pursued Mr. Fresne, "I distinctly heard it. I cannot bear the thought of an animal in distress."

Minerva hesitated. And then from the blackness of the shrubbery came a distinct *miaow.*

"There really *is* a cat!" exclaimed Minerva.

"So there is," cried Mr. Fresne, sending up a prayer of thanks to that God who looks after Dandies.

"Then we must certainly rescue it," said Minerva. She hesitated again. "Perhaps it is not in any difficulty at all but simply just miaowing to . . . to pass the time."

At that the unseen cat gave a terrible strangled cry and all Minerva's doubts fled. She plunged into the undergrowth followed closely by Mr. Fresne.

The bushes closed behind them, shutting out the lights of the party, enclosing them in warm darkness.

"Miaow," said the cat, plaintively, from quite close by.

Mr. Fresne forgot about the cat. He was alone with Minerva in the warm darkness. He could smell the flower perfume she wore. He threw his arms around her and crushed her to his buckram-wadded chest.

"Mr. Fresne!" cried Minerva, struggling as hard as she could. "The cat!"

"A pox on the cat," said Mr. Fresne thickly. He imprisoned her chin in one large hand and his lips sought hers.

Mr. Fresne had thought the welcome darkness was due to the shrubbery. But the moon, which had briefly sailed behind a cloud, cruised out again, and he found himself looking down into the blackness of Minerva's furious eyes.

"Miaow," said a mocking voice at his ear.

There was something so very human about that last miaow that Mr. Fresne twisted his head round.

Lord Sylvester was sitting on the low branch of a tree, his head a little above Mr. Fresne's.

"Miaow," he said conversationally.

"Why you . . ." spluttered Mr. Fresne.

"Let Miss Armitage go," said Lord Sylvester lazily.

"How dare you trick me!" cried Mr. Fresne, releasing Minerva and immediately adopting a boxing stance. "Come down and fight, you coxcomb. I'll draw your cork for you."

He danced towards Lord Sylvester, jabbing with his fists, as if shadow boxing, fully expecting his lordship to drop from his branch in sheer terror.

Lord Sylvester studied his antics with some amusement and then suddenly his foot shot out and caught Mr. Fresne so hard in the chest that that surprised gentleman went hurtling back into the undergrowth with a tremendous crash.

"Please take my arm, Miss Armitage," said Lord Sylvester, climbing down easily from his perch and leading Minerva away. He held back branches for her and soon had her safely out on the walk again.

There was an ominous silence from the shrubbery behind.

"Perhaps he was hurt," ventured Minerva.

"Only in his dignity. You must learn not to wander into the bushes with strange gentlemen, Miss Armitage."

"I would not have gone had I not heard a cat in distress. And you were that cat, my lord."

"But you might have been tricked in any case. I had to teach you to be on your guard."

"There was no reason to give me such a cruel lesson," said Minerva hotly. "I was in no danger of going into the shrubbery with Mr. Fresne and in no danger of believing his story about a cat if it had not been for your assistance."

"We shall see," said his lordship pleasantly. "Do stop

trying to tear your arm away, Miss Armitage. Remember you enlisted my help. It will not do your reputation one whit of good to be seen struggling with me.''

''Where are you taking me?''

''We are merely going for some refreshment. Now you must appear quite enchanted by my company.''

''But that will surely repel a possible suitor.''

''Not a bit of it. I am very fashionable, you know.''

''And smug.''

''And honest. Come, we are ruining this delightful setting and your lessons are about to begin in earnest. First of all, you must imagine yourself madly in love with me . . .''

''My lord!''

''. . . madly in love with me. You tremble at my touch. You wish the night would never end. You wish all these squawking and giggling people would vanish and leave us alone with the night.''

''You are ridiculous.''

''Only practical. I am quite prepared to make a cake of myself . . . I beg your pardon . . . imagine myself equally in love with you.''

''Well . . . well . . . perhaps we could pretend. But not *too* much,'' said Minerva nervously. ''I must find a suitor, you know.''

''You will. Everyone loves competition.''

He pushed open the glass door of the hothouse. The air was sticky and humid and heavy with the scent of plants and flowers. A tiny fountain of champagne was surrounded by a group of noisy young people.

''Don't drink that,'' said Lord Sylvester. ''It's bound to be flat. It uses the same champagne over and over again.''

He skilfully found them a small table in a corner, two plates of delicacies, wine for himself and a glass of ratafia for Minerva.

She sipped the almond-flavoured liqueur and looked about her with interest.

''It is most odd,'' she remarked. ''I was taught that everywhere I went in London society, I would find rigid manners and decorum. But here . . . everyone seems so abandoned somehow. Some of the ladies are very drunk and most of the chaperones are absent."

"The secret is not in how one behaves. The secret is not to be found out in a misdemeanour. *That* society will never forgive. Minerva, your eyes are great dark pools in the lamplight and your hair glows like the raven's wing."

"It's no use trying," said Minerva. "I feel embarrassed."

"*You* are not trying. *I* have convinced myself for the moment that I am in love with you and find it all very pleasurable. Look at me!"

Minerva looked into his eyes. How very green they were!

"Now, no one is watching. Take my hand."

Almost hypnotised by that steady green gaze, she held out her hand and felt it enclosed in his long fingers.

He gently ran his thumb across her palm.

"I love you, Minerva," he said.

Minerva felt giddy. She seemed to be whirling around and around in a dizzying vortex of emotions. Somewhere deep inside her a little voice was crying, "Oh, if only he meant it."

"You pretend the state of love very well," she said breathlessly. "I thought you had never been in love."

"No. Not what I would call love. I like some spirituality about my sensuality else nothing will exist when all passion is spent."

He slowly rolled her white kid glove down her arm and then, holding her hand prisoner, bent and pressed his lips against the wildly beating pulse at her wrist.

Her other shaking hand automatically seemed to take on a life of its own, to reach out to caress his thick brown-gold hair, and then alarm bells began to go off in her head.

Such feelings were sinful. This man was a hardened rake who had surely played this game time and time again. She wrenched her hand away and then buried both hands in her lap and stared at him defiantly.

"You are a difficult case," he murmured. "Eat your food."

To Minerva's surprise, he began to talk lightly of this and that, becoming again a cool and elegant stranger. Again she experienced that strange feeling of loss and found to her surprise that she was beginning to flirt a little, laughing at his stories, and trying to amuse him with stories of her own.

"Lady Godolphin is really rather a good soul," said Minerva. "All her bold remarks and strange dress are simply part of an act."

"You must not believe that," he said, spearing a wafer of Westphalia ham with his fork. "Lady Godolphin is kind in her way but she has absolutely no morals whatsoever and never had any either. If you believe anything else, you will be in for a shock."

"My father would not have sent me to her if she is as bad as you say," replied Minerva. "I know that he sometimes appears more of a huntsman than a clergyman, but he would not for a moment condone . . ."

"He has not seen Lady Godolphin since he was a young man and she was a frivolous beauty celebrating her first widowed state. Yes, you may stare with those enormous eyes of yours. But my father assures me that Lady Godolphin was the prettiest thing in London at one time. But to return to us. If you have quite finished, we will stroll back to the ballroom." He tilted his head a little and listened to a faint fanfare of trumpets. "The Prince Regent has arrived."

"Oh, I *must* see him. My family will want to know all about him. They would never forgive me if I missed him."

"Then we must hurry," he smiled, putting his napkin down beside his plate.

"He only means to stay about fifteen minutes. He has been reported as feeling poorly, but even he must attend when the Countess summons."

When they were back out in the walk, following the hurrying throng in the direction of the striped marquee which acted as ballroom, he started to guide her away from the walk and across a narrow path leading through the dark shrubbery.

"Don't be alarmed, Miss Armitage," he teased. "I am

merely taking you the quickest way. We shall enter by the far door and that way avoid the crush at this end.''

''You called me Minerva before,'' Minerva found herself saying.

''Ah, but that was when I was in love with you. That was when, for one moment, your dark eyes shone like stars reflected in a lake. You have the most fascinating eyes, Minerva. In daylight, they are grey, like winter water, in the dusk, they are silver, and at night, they are dark. I would like to see those stars shine again. What can I do to light them in your sky?''

They were nearing the end of the path and the noise of the orchestra and the chatter of voices sounded clearly on the evening air.

Before she could guess what he was about to do, he had taken her lightly by the upper arms and had swung her around so that she fell against him.

''Let me go, my lord,'' she whispered. ''I shall scream.''

''No. You will kiss me.''

''My lord, I . . .''

''Kiss me, Minerva.''

The voice was deep and caressing. His eyes glinted in the moonlight and a faint smile curled his beautiful mouth.

His hard body pressed against her own was doing terrible things to her senses. She began to feel as if her body had melted and was hotly fusing with his own. His hand caressed the back of her neck and she let out a low choked sound like a moan.

''Afraid to kiss your brother, your mentor?'' he teased. ''Come, Minerva, my love, you are sorely in need of practice. And who's to see us?''

''Someone might.''

''Only the moon.''

''Let me go,'' entreated Minerva again, frightened by all the strange raging cravings which were assaulting her.

''Then kiss me.''

''Oh, very well,'' said Minerva, screwing up her face and jabbing a kiss on his mouth with pursed lips. But somehow his mouth seemed to cling to her own, and, despite herself, she felt her lips softening, answering the deepening pressure of his own.

And then she simply lost any idea of time and space. She was whirling around and around in a warm, dark sea and she never, ever wanted to come to land again.

When he finally released her, the shock was so great that she shivered, and looked up at him with wide drowned eyes, wondering at the sudden strange expression in his, a sudden look of . . . awareness? Apprehension?

"Have you ever danced the waltz?" he asked, tucking her arm in his and beginning to walk towards the ballroom.

"N-no."

"Would you like to try?"

"Don't know," mumbled Minerva, wondering how he could sound so calm.

They reached the entrance to the ballroom, blinking in the bright light from hundreds of candles.

"Sylvester!"

Lord Sylvester muttered something under his breath. A voluptuous redhead stood facing them, all glittering smile and hard eyes.

"Miss Armitage, may I present Mrs. Dattrey. Miss Armitage is newly come to Town."

"And has been wandering in the moonlight with the wicked Sylvester? Shame on you, my lord. 'Tis not like you to pursue young innocents."

Lord Sylvester put up his quizzing glass and studied Mrs. Dattrey's painted face. "You are right," he said with a little sigh, letting the glass fall. "I usually confine my attentions to harlots."

"Why, Sylvester," exclaimed Mrs. Dattrey with a shrill laugh. "You are really very angry."

Minerva wrenched her arm from Lord Sylvester's grasp and stalked off in the direction of the chaperones, her face flaming. That awful woman. She had called him Sylvester. And the way she had looked at him had suggested a very close relationship. And he had said he usually only consorted with harlots. He had admitted it! And she had let such a man handle her intimately. Before she could reach Lady Godolphin's side, fat and florid Harry Blenkinsop came up to solicit her hand for the waltz. Minerva at first was too furious and too shaken to explain that she did not know how to perform the dance.

She let him lead her onto the floor and gasped with alarm as his arm circled her waist. "I cannot do this dance!" she cried.

"Oh, it's simple," he wheezed. "Just follow me."

Minerva tried not to stumble as she was whirled around and around. He was pumping her arm energetically up and down in time to the music and she could feel her flimsy skirts billowing out about her legs. She was glad she had worn a pair of blue silk garters, thoughtfully provided by Lady Godolphin.

It was disgraceful that one's garters should show, but as Lady Godolphin had pointed out, if they *did* show, then they may as well look pretty.

Nonetheless, Minerva felt the dance was quite scandalous. Although Mr. Blenkinsop held her the regulation twelve inches away, Minerva could not but feel that the waltz was *fast*. Also a great number of ladies at the ball appeared to be in a state of semi-nudity. Minerva felt that the whole of London was hell-bent on displaying as much naked flesh as possible. As the *Satirist* put it: "the very Abigails have divested themselves of every petticoat, in order that the footman or valet may discover the outline of their secret beauties through a transparent calico."

Her distress was aggravated by the sight of Lord Sylvester twirling expertly with a handsome woman in his arms, and then by the amazing picture presented by Lady Godolphin who was spinning around with Colonel Brian like a dervish and displaying to the world a pair of muscular calves embellished with flesh coloured silk stockings and scarlet garters.

Pride came to her rescue. Lord Sylvester must not see how much his philandering had upset her. She must be grateful that her eyes had again been opened to his sinfulness.

And Minerva was so relieved to find that she did not care for Lord Sylvester one little bit that she flirted and laughed and talked to Harry Blenkinsop at a great rate while his cronies watched enviously from the edge of the floor.

"I wouldn't have thought Harry would've been the one to charm her," said Mr. Jeremy Bryce while Lord Chumley bleated his agreement.

But Silas Dubois tapped the side of his large nose and winked. "She ain't interested in him at all," he sneered. "It's Lord Sylvester Comfrey she's trying to impress. They've had some sort of row and she's determined to show Comfrey that she don't care a rap for him. By the way, have you heard what's all over Town? Seems Miss Armitage was playing a vast joke on society with all that priggish business."

"What!" His two companions looked outraged. Then Lord Chumley tried to look wise. "I knew it was all a hum," he said. "That's why I took against her so. Don't like that sort of behaviour in a female. T'ain't feminine."

Mr. Fresne meanwhile had been brushed and restored to his former glory. He could not bring himself to tell his two friends, Lord Barding and Sir Peter Yarwood, of his humiliation. But he did tell them of Minerva's remarks about Dandies.

"Faith!" exclaimed Lord Barding looking down at his salmon pink coat—or as much as he could see of it over the frozen torrent of starched muslin which made up his cravat. "She is a deuced odd female. But word has it she has been making a game of us all. She was teasing you, mark my words."

"No," said Mr. Fresne, glowering at the spectacle presented by the waltzing Minerva. "She was to all respects a very charming girl apart from that remark. She meant it."

"Well," put in Sir Peter Yarwood complacently, "Barding and I are out of the running so we don't need to trouble."

"I say," said Mr. Fresne, "if the bet's off, I don't really see why I should go on with it."

"A new bet!" cried Barding. "Yarwood and I will lay you 10,000 pounds that you can't get her to fall in love with you."

"Agreed!" said Yarwood gleefully. "Barding and I will

lend you our support. Think on't. You've always been a favourite with the ladies.''

So Mr. Fresne glowered and thought.

Minerva danced on. She was relieved when it at last came to an end. All at once she remembered to look for the Prince Regent, hoping that she had not missed getting a glimpse of him. Lady Godolphin was sitting on a cane chair at the wall being fanned by her elderly cavalier.

"Where's the Prince Regent?'' asked Minerva, having escaped from Harry Blenkinsop.

"Oh, over there,'' panted Lady Godolphin, waving her fan. "He's with Alvaney and Brummell.''. Minerva followed the pointing fan and saw a fair, fat and florid man who appeared to have been stuffed into his evening clothes. He was wearing the Order of the Garter across his plump chest. But Minerva only saw the power and the glory and was awed by her first glimpse of royalty. The Prince was laughing loudly at something Brummell had said. Then he and his party of friends moved towards the entrance of the tent. He stood for a few moments chatting with the Countess Lieven. And then he was gone.

Minerva let out a sigh of pure pleasure, her pain and humiliation momentarily forgotten. What a letter she would have to write home.

Home!

All at once she remembered the purpose of her Season and a shadow crossed her face.

A tall gentleman came up to claim her hand for the next dance. Out of the corner of her eye, Minerva saw Lord Sylvester asking another of those mature, handsome women to dance. She gave a little toss of her head and set herself to enchant her partner.

Lady Godolphin watched Minerva's progress with amazement and delight.

"That's young Chester she's dancing with,'' she said to Colonel Brian. "He's got quite a fortune. Who would have thought our prim Minerva would turn out so ravished?''

"Ravishing,'' corrected Colonel Brian. "Just like you, fair lady.''

Minerva danced and danced until her feet hurt and her ankles ached. She danced until the rosy dawn dimmed the light from the lamps. Not once did Lord Sylvester come near her. But he would surely call. One's partners were supposed to call to present their compliments the day after the ball.

But after the Aubryns ball he had simply sent a card by his servant. One did not need to call in person. So perhaps he might not. And she did not care.

Lord Sylvester was still angry with himself and with Minerva. He had been rude to that idiot, Mrs. Dattrey, and he had not meant to give that irritating lady such a set down. He was angry with Minerva for having walked away.

Finally his anger cooled. He decided to go and be as pleasant as possible to Mrs. Dattrey. And if it annoyed Minerva, then perhaps he could hope. Hope for what? demanded a startled little voice in his brain. He hesitated, shrugged, and made his way towards Mrs. Dattrey.

Minerva saw him and could only be glad that Lady Godolphin had decided that they must leave.

Lady Godolphin was quite tipsy but full of praise for Minerva. "I declare you are a good girl and a virtuous one," she said warmly. "You may read to me every night before I sleep."

A little of the pain at Minerva's heart eased at her words. Lord Sylvester had been wrong about Lady Godolphin. She was merely eccentric and not the wicked rip that Lord Sylvester had claimed her to be.

Lady Godolphin said "good night" as soon as they reached home but declared herself too excited to sleep a wink although it was already six-thirty in the morning.

After Minerva had been made ready for bed by Lady Godolphin's maid, she found herself too upset to sleep. She tossed and turned for about an hour, listening to the sounds of the waking streets.

She decided it would perhaps be a good idea if she went to Lady Godolphin's chamber and, if that lady were awake, she would read to her, and that would soothe them both.

Picking up a book of poems, Minerva pulled on her wrapper, and quietly made her way along to Lady Godolphin's rooms. She hesitated outside the door, listening. There was the sound of Lady Godolphin's voice coming faintly through the panels.

Minerva smiled. Poor, funny old thing, talking to herself. She scratched gently at the panels of the door.

"Who is it?" screamed Lady Godolphin.

"It is I! Minerva."

"Go away!"

"Now I know what is best for you," said Minerva in governessy tones. "I will enter and I will read to you until you sleep."

"No . . ." began Lady Godolphin, but Minerva pushed open the door.

There seemed to be a great thrashing and heaving of blankets.

Minerva lit a candle on the toilet table and carried it over to the bed.

Lady Godolphin stared at her wildly. The bedclothes were heaped up around her in an untidy mountain.

"Go away," said Lady Godolphin firmly. "Leave me alone, Minerva."

"Now, now," chided Minerva, pulling a chair up next to her. "I often read to Mama or my sisters when they cannot sleep. There is some very fine poetry in this volume. Now I shall begin:

> *" 'Hark! forward away, my brave boys*
> *to the chase.*
> *To the joys that sweet exercise yields;*
> *The bright ruddy morning breaks on us*
> *apace . . .' "*

Here Lady Godolphin let out a wild giggle and slapped at the bedclothes.

"Let me arrange your bedclothes for you," said Minerva, standing up.

"No!" screamed Lady Godolphin.

"Very well," said Minerva, sitting down again.

> *" 'And invites to the sports of the field.*
> *Hark! forward's the cry, and cheerful . . .' "*

"Your whole family would appear to be obsessed with hunting. Go away, Minerva. I am sleepy," said Lady Godolphin in a very angry voice.

Minerva looked at her doubtfully. Lady Godolphin's eyes were bulging and a thin film of perspiration covered her face.

"If you are sure you are feeling the thing, ma'am," she said, reluctantly closing the book. "You appear to have a fever."

"In which case I am better left alone," snapped Lady Godolphin. "If you do not leave this instant, Minerva, I shall throw the chamber pot at your head."

"Forgive me, my lady," said Minerva apologetically. "I would not have upset you for the world. It was just . . ."

"Please go away," moaned Lady Godolphin.

Minerva blew out the candle and tiptoed to the door. The sun was shining brightly outside but the room was mostly in darkness because of the thick curtains and shutters at the windows.

She closed the door gently behind her and stood irresolute. Perhaps she should not have left. Lady Godolphin had looked strained and ill.

Perhaps she should send for the physician?

Minerva very gently opened the door a little to reassure herself. And nearly died of shock.

Colonel Brian's gray head was emerging from under the bedclothes.

"By Jove!" he said. "I thought to have died of suffocation."

"And I thought to have died of embarrassment," replied Lady Godolphin. "Could you not have kept your hands still until she left? Crawling all over my body like that. If that missish miss thought I had had carnival knowledge of you, she would have fainted on the spot."

"If you mean carnal knowledge, I ain't had it yet. Come here and kiss me, you delicious creature."

There came a great deal of sucking noise, rather like a drain being unstopped.

Stricken, Minerva closed the door very, very gently. Very quietly she crept back to her own room and buried her burning face in the pillow. She could never bear to look at Lady Godolphin again. She must leave. Papa would not let her stay in such a household.

How could *anyone*, let alone a woman of Lady Godolphin's years . . . ?

Unbidden, the thought of Lord Sylvester's hard body pressed against her own flew into her mind.

And quite suddenly, Minerva began to cry.

Chapter Eight

The clear light of a new day did little to alter the plots and schemes of Minerva's ill-wishers. Mr. Fresne was burning with humiliation over the blow he had received from Lord Sylvester, and he used this resentment to rouse his friends, Yarwood and Barding, to further plans for Minerva's humiliation.

The company of four were urged on in *their* plots by the energetic Mr. Silas Dubois. Mr. Dubois really now wanted revenge on Lord Sylvester more than Minerva, but he kept this fact to himself. Lord Sylvester was everything that Mr. Dubois longed to be and could not achieve. He was popular, a first class sportsman, and a prime favourite with the ladies. To humiliate and disgrace Minerva, Mr. Dubois felt sure, would upset the elegant Lord Sylvester since that gentleman had seen fit to appoint himself a sort of guardian to Minerva.

The seven called in person at Hanover Square to present their compliments, the three Dandies attired in very sober clothes, only to find that Minerva had gone out walking with Lord Sylvester.

All began to wonder if Lord Sylvester might be considering marriage for the first time in his life.

It says a great deal for the anguish of Minerva's mind that she had accepted Lord Sylvester's invitation. She had only slept a few hours and had awoken with a miserable feeling of isolation and doom. She was deeply shocked by Lady Godolphin's conduct and felt she could never face her again. And as for Lord Sylvester, he was all part and parcel of this wicked immoral London society. Had he not admitted to consorting with harlots? Had his kiss which had so delighted and seduced her senses meant nothing more than a pleasant game to him?

She had dressed, and was just about to sit down and pen a letter to Lady Godolphin and to order the servants to pack her trunks when Mice, the butler, told her Lord Sylvester had called.

Lonely and despairing, Minerva forgot that only a moment before she had been castigating him in her mind as a rake, and immediately thought of him as her only friend in a wicked world.

She had burst into tears at the sight of him, saying she could not stay in this evil house a moment longer. He had told her quietly and firmly to fetch her mantle and bonnet and then had led her from the house.

He had driven her to the gates of Hyde Park and had told his tiger to guard the horses while he helped Minerva to descend.

"A walk is just the thing for you," he said.

The day was a sort of uniform grey; a typically English day. A soft grey sky stretched over the Park and a damp, humid wind ruffled the grey waters of the Serpentine.

At last he drew her down beside him on a bench and took her hands in his.

"Now," he said.

Minerva tried to talk but began to cry instead. He sat quietly until she had recovered, removing the small damp wisp of lace which served as a handkerchief and replacing it with a more serviceable one of his own.

After a few hiccups, Minerva choked out the tale of Lady Godolphin's wickedness.

Lord Sylvester bit his lips to repress a smile.

"And Colonel Brian is *married*," wailed Minerva. "She is committing adultery."

"Well, it is all very bad," he said. "The thing that amazes me is that her ladyship should not be more careful. I mean, to calmly let you observe . . ."

"Oh, she didn't." And Minerva with many blushes told him of reading to Lady Godolphin while Colonel Brian was hidden under the bedclothes.

Lord Sylvester put up a long hand to cover his face. He tried to stifle his laughter, but found he could not. At last he gave up the struggle, and simply roared with laughter, declaring through gasps that it was better than a farce.

Minerva's distress and embarrassment melted before a sudden burst of fury.

"You are all just as bad," she raged. "Immoral, sinful, licentious . . ."

"Stop!" said Lord Sylvester, mopping his eyes with another handkerchief which he dug out of the pocket in the tails of his coat.

"Look, my love, you will understand these things when you are older. Lady Godolphin is very kind to make the effort to bring you out this Season. Her morals are bad . . . but yours are not. Quite a lot of ladies behave so and nobody minds so long as they are discreet. Don't glare at me. Is Lady Godolphin unkind? Does she beat her servants? No. You cannot change other people, Minerva. Try for a little more tolerance. I shall return with you, so that when you face Lady Godolphin you will have me to support you. It is best to ignore the whole thing."

"I never thought I would miss Hopeworth so much," said Minerva in a low voice.

"But you are newly come to Town. Is it not too early to feel homesick? A young lady like yourself has so many amusements in town compared to the quiet life of the country."

"London shocks me," said Minerva slowly. "Oh, I am not going to moralize. But I had always pictured London as a sort of Camelot—all towers and spires floating in the light of a clear day. Courtesy, honour and wit. I find a

great many of the members of society downright boorish.
And the very air! I can hardly breathe in the close atmosphere and the sewers smell so very horrible. The bread is
sour, the meat is tough, the water is filthy and the milk is
blue. We have our amusements at Hopeworth. We make
the very most of local events you know; sheep-washing
and sheep-shearing, throwing a big old tree, the village
club feast, harvest home, and the burning of a big bacon
pig . . .''

"The *what?*"

Minerva smiled. "How rustic I must sound. We have a
village pig-burner, old Mr. Toms, who takes a big pig of
about twenty score and with the aid of layers of straw, he
singes all the hair off the dead pig without scorching its
hide and turns it out like a beautifully coloured meer-
schaum.''

"You have no theatre, no opera?"

"We have the mummers at Christmas. There's always St.
George, with a real sword, the King of Egypt, whom he
slays, and the Doctor who cures everything. I believe the
plays are very old. And I feel *needed* there. I could help people.''

"You cannot live through other people all your life," said
Lord Sylvester.

Minerva wanted to reply, "I don't know what you mean.
One is supposed to live for others," but instead she found
herself asking, "Was it you who sent me that poem, and the
flowers?''

"It is the change from country to city that has shaken
you," he said, gazing out over the green expanse of the Park
to where a herd of cows grazed peacefully, and seeming not
to have heard her question. "After some time here, you will
find the country very flat.''

"Then I should have lost my values.''

"And gained some honesty. It is all very well thinking
what you ought to think, but that only carries you along for a
certain length of time. It is good for the soul to be honest
with yourself.'' His green eyes were now glinting down at
her. "Now, would it not be terrible if you were in love with
me and your intellect told you to repulse me?''

"No, it would not be so very terrible at all. Especially after last night, my lord, when you declared you found your pleasures with *harlots*."

"Yes, I was very rude and did not mean a word of it. Mrs. Dattrey annoyed me excessively. My soul was full of romance and moonlight and the memory of a warm pair of lips . . ."

"I would like to go home, my lord," said Minerva, rising quickly to her feet and brushing down the folds of her gown.

"You must learn to counter such remarks if they embarrass you and not run away," he said severely. "If you do not like the gentleman who is paying you compliments or reminding you of something you would rather forget, then you simply change the subject."

"As you did when I asked you if you had sent the poem and the flowers?" said Minerva, looking down at him.

He rose to his feet. "Since you are standing, I must stand also. If, on the other hand, you are attracted to the gentleman who is paying you compliments but feel his conversation to be a trifle too warm, you blush and hang your head and flutter your fan, and say, "Oh, please don't," in a sort of breathless voice. It's all part of a game. You *do* want to be married, do you not?"

"I want to save my family from the debtors' prison," exclaimed Minerva, throwing her head and staring nobly into the middle distance.

"Such nobility! Such sacrifice," mocked his lordship.

"Something which you, my lord, certainly don't understand."

"Oh, but I do . . . when it is the genuine article. Come along, Minerva, let us go and confront Lady Godolphin. Tell me about these brothers and sisters of yours as we go along."

Minerva bit her lip, but the temptation to talk about her beloved family was too strong.

"Well, they are marvellous children and I love them dearly. Of course, Annabelle cannot be considered a child any longer for she is turned sixteen." Unself-consciously,

Minerva took Lord Sylvester's arm. "Annabelle is *very* pretty. Papa said that fair girls were not the crack, but she would have had better success in London than I. She flirts very prettily."

"And with whom has the fair Annabelle been flirting?"

A shadow crossed Minerva's expressive little face. "Oh, but it was all rather dreadful. It appeared she was to be affianced to Lady Wentwater's nephew—Lady Wentwater being our neighbour, you know—but it turned out he was a *slave trader.*"

"Ah, so you had an opportunity to see her flirt. Did the good vicar ban the marriage?"

"Oh, it never got to *that*. We all just *cringed* from Mr. Wentwater, including Annabelle. After we heard of his trade, there was no question of marriage."

"And the others?"

"Then there's Deirdre who is fourteen. She is very naughty and clever—always dressing up. Very intelligent and mischievous. Then there is Daphne and after her, Diana, and then little Frederica. The boys, Peregrine and James, are splendid little fellows. They are identical twins and I declare I am the only one who can tell them apart. . . ."

And so Minerva chattered on, hanging on to Lord Sylvester's arm and turning her glowing face up to his.

Mr. Silas Dubois moved slightly behind a tree trunk and studied the pair as they strolled towards the gates of the Park. He was overcome by such a hatred of Lord Sylvester that he quite shook, and his lordship slightly turned his head in Mr. Dubois' direction as if he had picked up the antagonistic waves sent out towards him.

Minerva had never had such a good listener in her life before. Talking about her family restored her confidence and made her feel as if she might be able to cope with this wicked world. And when she entered the Green Saloon and found Lady Godolphin looking quite normal—if Lady Godolphin could ever be said to look normal—she was able to greet her with an aplomb which surprised herself.

Lady Godolphin was full of the British success in taking Ciudad Rodrigo, praising Wellington to the skies, and hoping the Whigs were squirming. The Whigs had received a crushing blow when the Prince of Wales was appointed Regent the previous year. They presumed he had supported them in their belief that Wellington was a stupid blunderer and the war against Napoleon a waste of time. The Prince Regent in his opening speech had praised Wellington and damned the French.

Her view of the battle was, perhaps, a strange one and Lord Sylvester had to turn his head quickly away when Lady Godolphin enthusiastically described how the British had scaled the French "fornications."

It was all very foreign to Minerva. In Hopeworth, the villagers did not seem to be aware of the war. Spain was so very far away and Napoleon an ogre who had terrified them for so long that they had quite forgotten he was still a menace.

"But I do not understand," she cried. "If the French are so despicable, if we are at war with them, if we despise them so much, why then do we adopt their fashions and why does everyone in society interlard their conversation with French phrases?"

"I don't know," said Lady Godolphin. "But *chaçun à son goat*, as we say at St. James's."

"*Gout,*" corrected Minerva, weary of her hostess's malapropisms.

"Goo where?" demanded Lady Godolphin in surprise.

"Miss Armitage was merely wondering if you had any social engagements this afternoon," said Lord Sylvester maliciously.

"Not for this afternoon," replied Lady Godolphin with a puzzled look at Minerva. "You must be very careful not to let your accent slip, Minerva. Go, not goo. Rustic voices are not the thing."

"Very well, my lady," said Minerva, throwing a cross look at Lord Sylvester whose shoulders were shaking with laughter.

"Now I must lie down for a nap before this evening. I am quite exhausted with all my activities," said Lady Godolphin without a blush. "I trust you will behave yourself, Comfrey?"

She waddled out.

"You should not encourage her," said Minerva severely. "Her language is appalling. French fornications indeed."

"I think her ladyship meant fortifications."

"Oh."

"You have such a wicked mind, Minerva."

"That is not true. Now if you will excuse me . . ."

He bent over her hand and kissed it and stood holding it looking down into her eyes. She felt that strange melting feeling. Overcome with an agonizing longing to throw herself into his arms, Minerva fought it by rudely snatching her hand away and walking over to the fireplace and standing with her back to him.

And yet she was even angrier when she at last turned around and found that he had gone.

Two days after Minerva's discovery of Lady Godolphin's adultery, a calm sunny morning arose over the village of Hopeworth.

Annabelle stretched her long limbs and turned over in her mind what she should wear to church. She felt sure Guy Wentwater would be present, even though he had not put in an appearance at Evensong during the week. Although Josephine and Emily were to leave for London on Monday so that they could be present at Almack's opening ball on the Wednesday, she wanted to see if she could reanimate Guy's feelings towards her. It would be infuriating to find that either of Sir Edwin's daughters had secured him as a beau.

Annabelle was weary of household and parish duties and wished Minerva had not set such a precedent. There were the calls, the parish bags of bedclothes and linen to be made up for the poor and kept on hand for sickness, there was the household budget to balance, Annabelle's unformed sprawling hand looking untidy under the neat lines of Minerva's crabbed script in the household accounts.

At last, attired in a pretty sprigged muslin, she shepherded the children together for Mrs. Armitage's languid inspection. Annabelle fretted in a sudden access of impatience as Mrs. Armitage sent the twins to clean their ears, and Deirdre to take her hair down again and braid it.

At last they were ready to take the short walk to the church.

There had been a shower of rain the night before and the new green grass rolled and glistened like silk. Cows stood placidly in puddles in the marshy pasture and a frisky breeze sent drifts of fading hawthorn blossom dancing down to a muddy grave in the waterlogged road. Annabelle had had to wear her pattens over her pretty shoes because of the mud; she wondered whether it would be possible to slip them off before they reached the church.

All Annabelle heard at the vicarage from morning till night was money, or rather, the lack of it.

She was weary of pinching and scraping when the sale of one of Papa's splendid hunters would have relieved the strain. She longed for pretty things and sophisticated surroundings. Guy was rich, Guy was handsome, Guy could provide all those delights.

Annabelle began to wonder if she had been too top-lofty in repulsing him. The conscience that had screamed at her that he had been a slave trader was becoming drowned under the clamouring desire for some money and security.

The church was chill and damp after the sunshine outside. There were the usual rustics touching their forelocks as they shuffled past Squire Radford's pew; a host of old men and women in the body of the church who could not read and always looked at their Books of Common Prayer with expressions of blank amazement; and a lot of hobble-de-hoys of farm boys in the gallery. The choir was, as usual, accompanied by the blacksmith on the big bass viol, the barber on the clarinet, the miller on the bassoon, and the baker on the flute, all ready to lead the congregation through some of the Sternhold and Hopkins Old Version of the Psalms.

Marble plaques in memory of dead Armitages and Radfords shone palely in the light streaming through the long glass windows. The stained glass had been shattered by the soldiers of Henry VIII and had never been replaced. One brave fragment remained at the top of the chancel window, casting its prisms of harlequin light down onto the rich altar cloth, embroidered by Minerva.

Josephine and Emily, seated beside their mother and father, were all fuss and feathers and wriggles and giggles. The Armitage family took up two pews, Mrs. Armitage shepherding the younger children into one and Annabelle with the older ones in another. Lady Wentwater was alone in her pew, across from the Armitages. Annabelle looked gloomily down at the muslin of her dress and tried not to feel disappointed.

She had automatically begun to go through the ritual of the service when she felt a slight prickling on her right cheek. She knew instinctively Guy had arrived.

She stole a glance under the shadow of her bonnet and flushed as she met his amused pale blue gaze.

Annabelle was not blessed—or cursed, whichever way you look at it—by Minerva's overactive conscience, and so she did not consider her thoughts sacrilegious.

She did not think her father a very devout man, and was at times cynically amused by his obsession for the chase. It would have surprised her very much to know that her father was, in his eccentric way, a pastor who cared more for his parishioners than most.

Still, she was not to be blamed for her ideas, for the vicar's speech from the pulpit was in his usual vein.

He started off with that well known text from Matthew, "Consider the lilies of the field, how they grow; they toil not, neither do they spin." From there he went on to point out that it was essential for man and beast to work hard. His hounds, for example, had earned their summer rest. Men should work like foxhounds, that is together and in concert.

"It is characteristic of foxhounds to aid each other. If one makes what he supposes to be a discovery, the rest rush to see if there is anything in it." And so in a muddled way, the vicar compared the villagers to the pack, urging them to be ready when the last great horn blew.

There was a murmur of approval from the less literate body of the congregation. This was something they could understand more than any of Minerva's high-flown sentiments.

When the service was over, Annabelle ushered her charges out in front of her to where her cousins and their parents, Sir Edwin and Lady Armitage, were standing among the sloping gravestones. Guy Wentwater came out with Lady Wentwater on his arm. He gave Annabelle a brief bow and then went to join Josephine and Emily.

"I wonder he dares show his face in church," hissed Deirdre. Annabelle muttered, "Do be quiet. He does not trade any more."

She comforted herself with the thought that Guy Wentwater had not joined her, for he must know he would receive a rebuff from her family. Annabelle once more found Guy attractive. She did not know she was competing with Emily and Josephine to such an extent that the very spirit of rivalry would have made any man seem attractive.

Annabelle straggled along at the end of the family party, feeling let down and depressed.

The freshness of the day was going and a thin haze was covering the sun.

"Pssst!"

Annabelle quickly turned her head and saw the grimy face of one of the village boys framed in the leaves of the hedge.

"What is it Jem?"

The boy silently held out a crumpled note and put it into Annabelle's hand.

Annabelle glanced furtively up and down the narrow road. The family party was well ahead and just about to turn a bend in the road.

Quickly she opened the note. "Dear A," she read. "I cannot speak to you in front of your family. Please meet me in the copse at the corner of the six-acre. G."

For a moment, Annabelle's heart sang like the lark above, and then plummetted to earth. It was one thing to be courted by a young man with the approval of one's family. But to meet him in this clandestine way was wrong. She wished Minerva was home. Minerva would not let her go and so would take the decision out of her hands. But it was Sunday, and Minerva was in London and probably attending church. . . .

Poor Minerva found her first visit to a London church very strange. It seemed more like a rout than a religious service. She and Lady Godolphin were lucky in that they could simply walk across the square and did not have to wait while their coachman queued up in the press. The fashionable dress of the ladies, the singing, the loud sound of the organ, the distraction caused by a certain elderly lord who sang in a high cracked voice, quite off key, and whether anyone else was singing or not, and the constant *flirtatious* undercurrent as eyes peeked over the edge of prayer books among the young people, and the loud snores which came from the elderly made the service seem very strange indeed.

Her seven courtiers were there, however, and remarkably soberly dressed. They seemed to quite stun their acquaintances with their devout singing and their solemn attention to the service. They had decided that Minerva had not been making fun of society, but was as strait-laced as they had first thought.

Outside the church, after the service was over, they clustered about her, affording Minerva many envious glances from the other females and much irritation to herself. Try as she would, she could not find any of them attractive, even the smouldering Mr. Fresne.

To add to her consternation, Lady Godolphin invited them all back for wine and biscuits. But she followed Lord Sylvester's instructions and flirted as best she could. For she must marry somehow. Her family demanded it of her. And the boys' school fees must be paid.

Three of her other partners of the night before called to pay their compliments, but were outflanked by the seven who moralized so much that Minerva was in danger of losing her social reputation again.

They finally left. Minerva felt tetchy and irritable. To ease her mind, she read Lady Godolphin part of an improving volume called *Death Bed Scenes*, choosing one of her own favourites which was the tale of the Infidel Farmer.

At last it became evident to Minerva that Lady Godolphin was not listening. She put down the book with a sigh.

"My lady," ventured Minerva, "do you believe that those who commit adultery burn in the Eternal Fire?"

"I don't know," said Lady Godolphin, all puzzled innocence. "I've never thought about it."

"Think now," urged Minerva intensely.

The paint on Lady Godolphin's face creased into quite horrible wrinkles as she concentrated. She shook her head. "I don't know," she said again, "but when I get to hell, I'll let you know."

"My lady!"

"Minerva, you should not be thinking of such gloomy things. I think that with all these beaux, you will soon be wed. Why, we'll soon be thinking of your torso. I had a beautiful torso when I was married to Godolphin. All lace and satin, it was. Even my husband was wont to turn it over in his fingers and say he had never seen anything so fine."

"Do you mean trousseau, my lady?"

"Torso, trousseau, 'tis all the same. Lord Chumley is your best bet, I would say."

"He reminds me of a sheep."

"Most of 'em have something up with 'em. It's a pity Comfrey ain't the marrying kind. You'll have to make the best with what you've got. Chumley is comparatively young. You can fall in love *after* you marry. That's what most society women do."

But Minerva shook her pretty head. "When I am married, I will remain faithful to my husband, no matter what."

"Well, think about Chumley. Any woman can think herself into love if she puts her mind to it."

But can she think herself out of it? thought Minerva, suddenly depressed. Yet she could not be in love with Lord Sylvester. *She could not.*

With a little sigh, she made her excuses and went off to her room to write letters home. How immensely Annabelle would have enjoyed the Season! What a pity she isn't here instead of me, thought Minerva for the hundredth time.

belle would have enjoyed the Season. What a surprise. Come instead of him, thought Minerva, for the hundredth
time.

Chapter Nine

The vicar tilted his large head on one side and listened ap-
preciatively to the music of his hounds in their summer kennels. The hounds were apt to add singing to their other
performances, especially on a bright sunny day. Their
voices rose and fell in chorus and the vicar thought it the
sweetest music on earth.

Like Theseus, he thought his hounds: ". . . matched in
mouth like bells, Each under each, a cry more tunable Was
never hollo'ad to, nor cheered with horn."

The vicar was sitting on a tree stump at the edge of his or-
chard, lazily enjoying the morning weather.

There seemed signs that there might be a bumper harvest
after all. He thought briefly of his eldest daughter. He
should never have sent Minerva. She was vastly pretty, but
even her fond father had to admit to himself that she was
made to be an ape-leader.

Besides, he missed her already. Things did not run as
smoothly. The children always seemed to be squabbling. On
the other hand, he trusted Lady Godolphin to make sure that
Minerva married someone with money. For Lady Godolphin had always had a weakness for exacting monetary return. His conscience jabbed him at the thought of Minerva

dutifully married to a man she did not like. Then he comforted himself by thinking that that was the way of the world. He was sure his own wife did not like him overmuch. He thought of all the couples he had married who had stood before him at the altar, smelling of April and May, and who had been fighting like cat and dog before a year was up. The more placid ones seemed to settle down better.

"Mr. Armitage!"

The vicar looked up, annoyed to have his moment of quiet thought interrupted.

Mr. Pettifor, his curate, stood in front of him, the end of his long red nose twitching nervously.

"Yes, Pettifor, what is it?"

"I do not believe in tale-bearing," began the curate piously.

"Then don't," said the vicar reasonably. "Listen to those hounds, Pettifor. Celestial music, that's what it is. Celestial music."

"Yes, yes, Mr. Armitage. But I feel I must . . . I should . . . tell you. It concerns Miss Annabelle."

The vicar, who had been idly kicking a piece of turf with his boot, stopped, and looked up sharply at the curate, his eyes narrowed under the shade of the brim of his shovel hat.

"Annabelle, heh! Out with it then. Oh, come on. I'm *ordering* you, if that eases your conscience."

"On Sunday," said the curate, bending down and beginning to whisper, "Miss Annabelle was seen in the copse at the corner of the six-acre with Mr. Wentwater. On Sunday afternoon. They were seen in an amorous position."

Faint beads of sweat appeared on the vicar's brow, but he said in a level voice, "Be more explicit."

Mr. Pettifor looked down at him nervously. "Mr. Wentwater was . . . er . . . pressing her hand, warmly, and then he . . . kissed her on the mouth!"

The vicar removed his hat and mopped his brow.

"And how did Annabelle receive these attentions?"

"That is what was so terrible. She was laughing and flirting."

"And that's all there was? A kiss and a press of the hand?"

"Merciful Heavens! Your innocent. daughter! Is it not enough?"

"Oh, yes, yes. Who told you, Pettifor?"

"Young Jem Parsley."

"Ah."

"Jem told me that earlier on Sunday Mr. Wentwater had given him a shilling to deliver a note to Miss Annabelle."

"Well, forget about it. Don't talk about it, Pettifor."

"But Mr. Armitage . . ."

"Forget about it, man. I'm going to call on Squire Radford. Not another word. I know how to handle my girls."

But I *don't,* thought the vicar, as he swung down from his horse a bare half hour later outside Squire Radford's house. Jimmy Radford had a daughter, as I recall. Doesn't do any harm to ask for advice before I horsewhip that young puppy and cause a scandal. And I never could manage Annabelle.

The squire was a gnarled, little old gentleman who had once been a great traveller. His cottage *ornée* was filled with marble from Italy and brass from India, silks from China, and carved cedar from the Lebanon. No one could clearly remember Mrs. Radford, and sometimes it seemed as if the squire had always been a bachelor. He led the vicar into the garden to a table under a spreading sycamore and sent his Indian manservant to fetch a bottle of port.

"You are worried, Charles," said the squire in his thin, high voice. He perched on a chair opposite the vicar, his thin, stick-like legs in their clocked stockings neatly crossed at the ankle, the sun winking on the silver buckles of his shoes. He wore an elaborately curled and powdered wig which dwarfed his small, wrinkled face.

The vicar leaned forward and tapped the squire on the knee. "I need your advice, Jimmy," he said. "It's about Annabelle."

"Let me see," said the squire, handing the vicar a glass. "You'll like this, Charles. Excellent port. Ah, yes, Annabelle. That's the one who was almost engaged to Lady Wentwater's nephew, but you discovered he had been slave trafficking and so it was off. If I remember, you did not have to say anything to Annabelle. She took against the young man herself.''

''Yes,'' said the vicar, sipping his port, raising his bushy eyebrows, and downing the rest in a sudden gulp. ''Ah, that's good. Yes, I will have some more. Worry gives me a thirst. Yes, well, she's been seen flirting with Guy Wentwater. Now, I'm a hot-blooded man and my first idea was to go around there and give him a horse-whipping.''

The squire raised his hands in horror. ''You cannot horsewhip a gentleman!''

''He ain't no gentleman.''

''Now, you are becoming overheated. It was as well you came to me first. You have of course, for some reason, rejected the idea of talking to your daughter, which seems strange.''

''Annabelle's bored. There's nothing more dangerous than a bored girl with a rich young man around. She'll be off to Gretna if I put a spoke in her wheel. She don't fancy him. Boredom's what makes her fancy him. I put my oar in and she'll fall in love with him.''

''I trust you are not deliberately trying to upset me by telling me this?'' said the squire.

''I wouldn't for the world . . .''

''No, of course not. I lost my daughter many years ago to a wastrel. She . . . Mary . . . was a very flighty girl. I was away from home a great deal and my wife spoiled her quite dreadfully. I found one time when I returned from my travels that she had become engaged to a highly unsuitable young man and I put a stop to it immediately. She told me she would run away with him so I locked her in her room. My wife—God rest her soul—thought the whole thing was too romantic for words. She helped Mary elope with this idiot. Well, they were married at Gretna, and finally came back south and settled in London. I refused to have anything to do with them. I sent Mary money because it appeared they were in dreadful straits. This fellow, Percy Fitzwilliam was his name, gambled to excess. Mary died in childbirth and this Fitzwilliam kept on trying to borrow money. I refused to see him or answer his letters. What happened to him, I do not know. It was many years ago, just before you took up the living. I am amazed you have not heard of this, Charles.''

''People don't gossip much to me,'' said the vicar. ''You have to be interested when people gossip. I'm sorry to open old wounds, Jimmy.''

''No, it is too long ago to hurt me now. But if I had handled it another way, had found a means to drive the young man away without letting Mary or my wife know, well, she might be alive today. That's my advice, Charles. Go for Wentwater.''

''And horse-whip him?''

''No, no. You must find some way to frighten him, humiliate him. Let me think. Help yourself to more port, Charles.''

The vicar did as he was bid. The sunlight dappled down through the leaves of the sycamore on the squire's wrinkled face. His soft-footed servant placed another bottle on the table and silently withdrew.

A little brook ran through the bottom of the garden to join the River Blyne, adding its soothing murmur to the sound of the wind in the leaves above the vicar's head.

He found himself wondering about Minerva's lustful thoughts. Perhaps there was hope. Good girls like Minerva channelled these thoughts directly into marriage and childbearing. But Minerva would be apt to scourge them out of her system. Perhaps he should have told her that such thoughts were natural.

The squire attracted his attention by giving a dry little cough.

''Tell me Charles,'' he said. ''We know that foxes are vermin. If you heard of a fox in the countryside, what would you do?''

''Why . . . hunt him down o'course, hunt him down!''

''Exactly,'' said the squire.

The vicar looked at his friend in amazement, and then his little eyes began to twinkle, and he slapped his knee.

''Gently, calmly,'' cautioned the squire. ''We must lay plans. . . .''

* * *

"We must make plans," said Lady Godolphin. She and Minerva were sitting a little apart on the grass at a *fête champêtre*, held in a Surrey meadow by Lord Chumley.

"Yes," said Minerva in a dreary little voice.

"You have got him on the hook very nicely," said Lady Godolphin in an approving voice. "I really did not think you had it in you. Chumley is quite a catch."

"I don't see anyone else exactly competing with me for his favours," pointed out Minerva.

"Ah! That's because they have all given up hope. You quite enchanted him at Almack's opening ball. I had thought Comfrey might have interfered, but he was too taken up with that dashing widow, Jane Carstairs."

"Yes."

"He is a steady fellow and you will become accustomed to his looks. Always marry a steady fellow. My first was not. Before two weeks were out, he was trying to get the marriage annulled on the grounds that it had not been consumed, but it had been, consumed right and tight down at Brighton. 'No one will believe you anyway,' I told him, and he knew that to be true."

"I had hoped perhaps some *other* gentleman," said Minerva, "might be interested, and several quite charming gentlemen have come to call, but there are always these three friends of Lord Chumley's there, or Mr. Fresne and his friends, and they contrive to drive anyone else away. Even Lord Sylvester," she added in a small voice.

"Oh, I don't think anyone in the world could drive Comfrey away once he put his mind to it. But he don't bother with young misses and never has. Just be grateful that his attentions brought you into fashion in a small way. You never sit out a dance now, and everyone knows Chumley held his party especially for you, for he's normally so clutchfisted concerning anything *not* to do with the gambling table. . . ."

"And you would have me marry such a man? If he is not generous then how will it benefit my family?"

"Oh, once you're married, I'll tell you how to get his claws off the money-bags. I've had years of practise."

"Yes, my lady," said Minerva wearily.

She gloomily watched the approach of Lord Chumley. He looked more like a bad tempered sheep than ever. His fair hair was hidden under a small, tight, curly, white wig, and his yellow eyes were alight with anger.

"I detest pushers—people who have not been invited and then invite themselves without so much as a by-your-leave. Comfrey comes riding in as cool as you please, says he was "just passing" and heard the music. I said it was a private party and he says, "Of course, I would not expect you to have any other kind," takes a glass of champagne and wanders in to join my guests. I've a good mind to have my servants throw him out."

"You can't," pointed out the worldly-wise Lady Godolphin. "He's too fashionable."

"I don't know why that should be," snapped Lord Chumley.

"Ask his tailor," yawned her ladyship. "Has Colonel Brian arrived?"

"He was not invited."

"This is a curst dull party," said Lady Godolphin. "I'm going to see if I can find someone amusing. You know the horriblest people, Chumley."

She hoisted herself to her feet and waddled off, leaving Lord Chumley to glare after her.

Then he recollected his campaign, and eased himself down on the grass beside Minerva and smiled at her in a way that he was sure was absolutely killing.

"I feel I am getting to know you very well, Miss Armitage."

"My lord?"

"Yes, I feel there is a bond between us." Lord Chumley took Minerva's hand in his and Minerva forced herself not to draw her hand away. She knew her face was turning red with embarrassment and annoyance, and she knew equally that Lord Chumley would think she was blushing with maidenly confusion.

"You know, I gave this party for you," murmured Lord Chumley, looking down at Minerva's thick lashes, fanning over her flushed cheeks, and feeling quite tender towards her. He had formed a plot of his own. He would go ahead with the kidnapping to please the others and then when Minerva chose him, he would stun them all by taking her in his arms and asking her to marry him. He could see it all, feel her body, weak with relief, pressing against his own.

"I feel," he said inching closer to her, "that in order to know someone really well, it is a good thing to see a bit of their family background, meet their parents. Do you not agree?"

"Yes, my lord." How hot the sun was, thought Minerva. If only she could escape. But she was going to marry him and, after that, there would be no escape.

"And so, I would be honoured if you would accompany me to visit them . . . my parents, I mean."

Minerva looked around. How carefree everyone else seemed. People were talking and sitting or walking. A small orchestra was playing charming tunes beside a small lake. The wind moved lazily through the heavy summer leaves of the trees. Lady Godolphin was looking in her direction, a look which seemed to be saying "Get on with it."

And then Lord Sylvester passed at a little distance with a pretty woman on his arm. He was flirting with her, teasing her, looking down into her eyes with that heart-wrenching smile of his.

"Yes. I'll go with you," said Minerva. "When?"

"I don't know," said Lord Chumley, thinking furiously of all the arrangements he must make.

"Then you will surely let Lady Godolphin know in any case," pointed out Minerva. "I could not go without her permission."

"Quite." Lord Chumley thought that somehow Lady Godolphin must not be told, but at that moment he couldn't quite think how to arrange it. He must ask the arch-plotter, Silas Dubois.

At that moment, one of his servants came up to report that it would be necessary to open up the reserves of champagne. The guests had drunk the first lot.

"It can't be possible," said Lord Chumley, crossly, looking at Minerva's empty glass as if she were responsible for having consumed the lot. "Excuse me, my dear, but you see how it is. If things are to be done properly, I must handle everything myself.''

His place was quickly taken by Sir Peter Yarwood who had hit on the idea of putting in a word on behalf of Mr. Fresne.

All three Dandies were as soberly dressed as churchmen. They had been invited because Mr. Silas Dubois had pointed out they were no threat at all. Fresne was the only one who was not married, and Minerva showed no sign of favouring his suit, and so the three acted as a deterrent to any other hopeful suitor. Sir Peter was even more limp and drooping than ever, as if the heat of the day had taken the starch out of him. But he was, in fact, feeling quite noble. He had worn nothing but dull, sober clothes since Mr. Fresne had told them of Minerva's aversion to Dandies. And although he would have liked to cut a dash at the party, he felt exalted at the idea of wearing such dreadful garments in the name of friendship.

In fact, the advent of Minerva had drawn the three conspirators so close that they had forgotten how savagely they used to compete and quarrel.

''I have come on behalf of one who sighs for you,'' said Sir Peter languidly. ''Pon rep, does he sigh!''

''Indeed,'' said Minerva in a dull voice.

''And he is not a Dandy, and we know how you despise the Dandies,'' said Sir Peter, waving a playful finger under Minerva's nose and nearly cutting the tip with the end of his long drooping, mandarin-like nail.

Lord Sylvester's fair companion let out a rippling laugh of amusement and Minerva nearly ground her teeth.

''I do not dislike Dandies,'' she said.

''But you told Mr. Fresne you despised them!''

''Oh, *that*,'' said Minerva with a shrug. ''I thought you were all making a game of me so I said I didn't like Dandies to see if you would all modify your dress accordingly. And you did. But it was wrong of me. I don't really care what anyone wears, one way or t'other.''

''Excuse me,'' gasped Sir Peter stumbling to his feet. ''I feel unwell. The heat . . .''

He tottered off. He did indeed feel unwell. Oh, buckram

wadding and nipped-in waist, oh high-heeled splendid boots and gleaming spurs, oh, youth-giving rouge and paint; all, all sacrificed for some vicious, silly chit who was making a game of them all. *Laughing* at them. For days, they had dressed like crows. For days Bond Street had been devoid of the pleasure of seeing the magnificent trio on the strut. The pain was agonizing. They had gone to Almack's opening ball dressed like country squires. Oh, agony! The fact that the three had been playing a trick on Minerva in the first place did not enter his tortured brain. And then somewhere in the depths of his agony, he savoured the dismay of his friends. Just wait till he told them!

Minerva sat quietly by herself. She knew someone would soon join her if she did not move quickly, and she had a longing to be alone.

She quickly arose to her feet and hurried away from the party until the chatter and music had faded behind her.

There was a stand of trees at the water's edge, on the other side of it, a small pebbly beach at the edge of the lake with one large flat stone. Minerva realized she could sit on the cool stone, be shielded from the rest of the party by the trees, and also from the sun by their shadow.

She sat down on the rock and pulled off her pretty Lavinia bonnet and put it on the ground beside her. She rolled down her gloves and let the wind play over her bare arms. Minerva was wearing a white muslin gown with a Vandyked hem and Roman sandals of bronze kid. For the first few moments, she savoured the coolness, the sense of freedom, the beautiful isolation. And then a wave of depression swooped down on her.

So many girls finished their Season without marrying. They were allowed to go home and try again the following year. But their families had money, and she had not.

She could write to her father and beg him to take her home. A description of Lady Godolphin's misconduct would surely be enough. Her father was not an ogre. But the boys would not get their schooling and her sisters would have no dowries and no future.

Minerva was afraid that her moral standards were slipping badly. She felt she should be unable to look at Lady Godol-

phin without blushing but that old lady seemed quite uncon-
cerned. Minerva often found herself thinking of kisses and
strong arms holding her close until her body seemed to ache
with longing. She tried to put Lord Chumley's face onto her
dream lover, but it kept fading to be replaced by a handsome
face with a pair of mocking green eyes.

"Dreaming of marriage?"

Minerva looked up into the very pair of eyes she had been
thinking about. Lord Sylvester smiled down at her. "I had a
devil of a job finding you," he said. "I couldn't ask anyone
or they might have come looking for you themselves."

"Why do you seek my company now, my lord?" said
Minerva harshly. "You have not troubled yourself with me
of late."

She thought of the opening ball at Almack's and how she
had dreamed of dancing with him and talking with him and
how he had not even asked her to dance once.

"Now, how do you know I have not been troubled?"

He was carrying a bottle of champagne and two glasses.
He sat down beside her and leaned over and put the bottle in
the water to keep it cool and balanced the two glasses on the
inside of her bonnet which was lying on the ground.

"You were supposed to have helped me in my debut,"
said Minerva, uncomfortably aware of his nearness. Her
whole side that was next to him seemed to be tingling, as if
every little cell were straining towards him. The calves of
her legs trembled and she clasped her hands firmly in her
lap.

"But you were doing so well! Society is quite enchanted,
although your court of seven seems to drive everyone away.
Still, I see you have settled for Chumley."

"Yes."

"What, what! I expected a heated denial. I had supposed
you were encouraging Chumley's attentions in order to
make some of the other men jealous."

"No."

"Such monosyllables. What would Lady Godolphin call
a monosyllable? Probably a monosyllabub. She would consider it a description of a single helping of pudding."

"It is hard to understand her sometimes," said Minerva,

staring out across the water, and fighting for calm. He must not know how much he disturbed her.

"But," he continued, "if you are going to throw yourself away on Chumley, then I suppose I must allow you to do so. Such sacrifice! I hope your family appreciates it."

"Lord Chumley is very kind. Also, I must marry soon. There is my family to care for. Lady Godolphin also expects me to pay her back for the expense of this Season."

"Odso! One would not think anyone so generous with her ageing favours as Lady Godolphin would be so mercenary. She is very rich, you know. Are you sure you are not mistaken?"

"No. She has made matters quite plain."

"And your father knew of this?"

"Yes."

"He did not strike me as a cruel or insensitive man."

"He is a *man*," said Minerva wretchedly. "And that is why he thinks women will be happy enough with a home of their own and children. You consider our sex something of a joke yourself, my lord."

"I' faith, you wrong me badly. I worship at your feet. I pursue you endlessly. I . . ."

"You are very cynical. You treat me as a child."

"You are little more," he said gently. "You must realize, Minerva, that, yes, marriage to someone you do not love can be quite all right, but to someone kind and trustworthy who will respect your wishes. But do consider the intimacies of marriage with a man like Chumley."

"It is not a woman's place to consider the intimacies of marriage," said Minerva. "That side of it is simply something that women have to endure. We do not have the same lusts and passions as men."

"No?" His arms went around her, pulling her round and pressing her tightly against his chest. He began to kiss her face very lightly; small, teasing kisses on her eyelids, her cheeks, the tip of her nose. She tried to summon all her will to repulse him, but her eyes looked up into his, wide and drowned, and her mouth trembled. He kissed her gently on the mouth then, made a slight movement as if to release her, muttered something and kissed her again . . . and again

. . . and again, until, with something like a groan, he pressed his lips down savagely over her own, forcing her mouth apart, biting the inside of her lip, exploring, bruising, his caressing hands beginning to wander freely over her shaking body.

"Comfrey!"

Very slowly he released Minerva and looked round.

Lady Godolphin was standing at the edge of the trees, her pudgy arms folded across her breast, her dumpy little figure holding a strange air of command and authority.

"I must ask you what your intentions are towards Miss Armitage, Comfrey?" said Lady Godolphin. "I'm waiting."

Lord Sylvester got to his feet and drew Minerva up with him. He walked a little way away from Minerva, looking back at her with a strained look on his face.

Then he turned to Lady Godolphin. "You ask me my intentions, ma'am. Well, they're the worst, damme! The very worst!"

And with that he strode away.

Lady Godolphin stumped down onto the beach and Minerva subsided back on the rock as if her legs would no longer hold her.

"He didn't touch your virginal, did he?" demanded Lady Godolphin crossly.

"If you mean, am I still a virgin, of course," said Minerva, in a shaking voice. "How dare you think I would let any man . . ."

Lady Godolphin plumped herself down on the rock beside Minerva. "Now, now, don't be in such a taking. There's no harm done, so I'll say no more." Whereupon Lady Godolphin began to say a great deal more, and at length, helping herself liberally from the bottle of champagne that Lord Sylvester had left cooling in the water.

She raged against Lord Sylvester, saying he could have any woman in London for the asking and why he was trifling with Minerva's affections, she was blessed if she knew. The man was charming, handsome, and a rake. A confirmed bachelor. He kept mistresses, a whole stable of 'em, just as another man might keep horses. But he certainly wasn't going to marry a country miss.

Minerva sat miserably with her head bowed. For one wild moment when he had been kissing her, she had felt that his passion was as great as her own. But he was practised in the art of seduction and probably knew to a nicety how to fake it.

And then somewhere at the pit of her misery, a warm glow started. She would forget about Lord Sylvester. She would marry Chumley. It would be the ultimate sacrifice. She let out a little sigh of relief. The road to duty lay straight and narrow before her.

She interrupted Lady Godolphin's tirade. "I am going to marry Lord Chumley, so you may rest easy. You will get every penny of your money back."

Like most mean people, Lady Godolphin was immediately on the defensive. That was not the reason she thought Minerva should marry. She, Lady Godolphin, was a poor widow woman, despite evidence to the contrary. She hardly knew how to make ends meet.

Minerva listened meekly to this defense, watching the sunlight glowing on the heavy diamond and ruby necklace around Lady Godolphin's fat and withered neck.

"Anyway, you should be grateful to me for taking you away from a dead-alive place like Hopeworth," ended Lady Godolphin. "You must admit nothing exciting ever happens *there!*"

Earlier that day, Mr. Guy Wentwater was speeding along the Cartham Road—the road that led south out of Hopeworth as opposed to the Hopeminster Road that led north. The yellow wheels of his high perch phaeton spun in a golden blur and the sun gleamed on the glossy flanks of his matched greys.

He was on his way to visit a remote branch of the Wentwater family who lived some thirty miles from Hopeworth.

He had planned this expedition carefully, its purpose being to make young Annabelle miss him. She had become a trifle complacent after Emily and Josephine had left for London, and Guy shrewdly guessed that she was getting too sure of him and therefore having second thoughts. She kept harping on about the slave trade. He was quite sure he could get her to elope with him. He had toyed with the idea of simply taking her away, but that would cause a scandal, and Lady Wentwater might cut him out of her will—and for all the money he gained, Guy always wanted more. He did not believe for one moment his aunt's pleas of poverty and considered her an old miser, which was very probably true. The weather had been splendid, the mugginess of the previous days having lifted. Great fleecy castles of clouds sailed majestically across the sky. The hedges were alive with birdsong.

Faintly on the wind, behind him, he thought he heard a hunting horn. He slowed his team to a canter. There it was again. The good vicar had gone quite mad, he mused. Whoever heard of a foxhunt at this time of year? It could not be possible. He slowed his team to a halt.

A great cry suddenly rang out over the countryside *"Gone away! Gone away! Forrard! Forrard!"*

"Quite mad," mused Guy, picking up the reins. But something made him twist his head and look down the long white ribbon of road stretched out behind him.

Racing, bunched together, in full cry, came the vicar's hounds. Guy swore under his breath. Best to sit still and hold his horses until they had passed. But the loud belling of the hounds struck some primitive chord in his heart and he shivered despite the warmth of the day.

He watched, hypnotized, as the pack surged towards him.

The thickset figure of the vicar on a huge hunter appeared behind the pack, waving his hat and yelling, "Yoicks!" for all he was worth. *"Yoicks!"* came the answering echo of John Summer, the whipper-in.

And then Guy froze in terror as he found himself surrounded by the leaping, snarling pack. His horses reared and plummetted.

"Mr. Armitage!" cried Guy in terror. "Call them off!"

"Stay!" shouted the vicar, riding up, and the hounds crouched down in a ring around the phaeton, lips drawn back over sharp fangs, red eyes glaring up at the quivering Guy.

"Step down, Mr. Wentwater," said the vicar, dismounting from his horse. "I would have a word with you."

"But they'll tear me apart!" screamed Guy.

"They will, if you stay there, and I don't know I can hold 'em that long. They won't touch you if you come down."

"My horses will bolt."

"John, hold Mr. Wentwater's horses," commanded the vicar. "Now, Mr. Wentwater . . ."

Guy climbed down and stumbled as his shaky legs bore him towards the vicar. The vicar put a paternal arm around his shoulders and led him a little down the road.

"I'm sorry about this, Mr. Wentwater," he said. "Y'see, though it's not the Season, the farmers have been plagued by this here fox, and when I hear of vermin on my property, I get rid of it. Now, this pack o'mine has taken agin you and I can't promise they won't tear you apart another time. Your visit to Lady Wentwater is at an end, so I am sure you won't be back in Hopeworth for some time. I mean, as it stands, the hounds'll tear you limb from limb. I'm sorry about it. But I don't like vermin on my land. D'you see?"

And Guy looked at the vicar, and he saw.

He tried to muster some dignity but his face was ashen and his whole body was trembling.

"I shall not be returning for some time," he said in a strange, high, shrill voice.

"Then we have nothing to worry about. You may be on your way, Mr. Wentwater."

Sweating and stumbling at every step, Guy made his way back to his carriage and swung himself up. The hounds had retreated some way down the road and were standing around John Summer.

The vicar swept off his shovel hat and made a low bow. "Goodbye Mr. Wentwater. We shall not be seeing you for some time."

Guy smiled, his lips curling back over his teeth in a travesty of the hounds' snarls. He cracked his whip and set off down the road at such a speed that after only a few moments there was nothing but a cloud of white chalk dust to mark his passing.

The vicar turned around with a broad grin on his face. "Let 'em have it, John, though 'tis so old and mangy, I hope it don't poison 'em."

John Summer winked and opened the sack under his arm and drew out the dead fox which had been hidden in the box under Guy Wentwater's carriage seat and hurled it into the nearby field where the hounds pounced on it. He had removed it from its hiding place in the phaeton when the vicar was talking to Guy.

"Pooh!" said John, holding his nose. "Wunnerful he didn't smell it."

"Ah, well," said the vicar cheerfully. "Them vermin never know when they're not wanted. It's been a good day, John, and I would like you to come with me to Squire Radford. He'll want to know all about it."

But:
"And I thought that would fetch you. I heard the got now. I had been in town above an hour. It's the fall style. Claims the discovery, tangled, right's my gir

Chapter Ten

"It's uncommonly kind of you to give me house room," said Peter, Marquess of Brabington, helping himself to another tankard of beer. "I never thought to enjoy the luxury of a quiet English breakfast again."

"Yes," said Lord Sylvester from behind the barrier of the *Morning Post*.

"I never thought to see another Season either. You've no idea the humiliation of being dumped aboard a hospital ship and taken home to England and all because of a severe bout of dysentery and fever. If they had left me alone, I would have been well enough to return to my regiment in a few days."

"Um."

"But now I *am* here, I shall have at least a month of peace and quiet far from the cannon's roar. It's a messy war, Sylvester. Damned Boney owns most of Europe and those Whigs don't see the point of all the British fighting."

"Quite."

"You are not listening to a word I say. You are probably not even reading that paper either but merely using it as a shield while you dream of the fair Minerva."

"What!"

"Aha! I thought that would fetch you. I heard the gossip before I had been in town above an hour. It's the talk of the clubs. There's this vicar's daughter who's got the most unlikely collection of beaux on a string—including you."

"Nonsense." Lord Sylvester put down his newspaper and looked at his friend with some exasperation. "You should know better than to listen to gossip like that, Peter. They've had me practically married off to one or t'other since I came out of short coats."

"This gossip had a different flavour to it."

"Take it from me, it's all a hum. How shall I entertain you? Do you wish to meet some pretty ladies?"

"Not I. I was never in the petticoat line. There's a prize fight down in Hopeminster I mean to attend."

"Hopeminster," said Lord Sylvester thoughtfully. "Perhaps I might join you. I had forgot all about it. This Saturday, I believe."

Lord Sylvester began to discuss the merits of the various pugilists and successfully diverted his friend's mind from Minerva.

Minerva, thought Lord Sylvester, while he chatted easily. *I can't get that wretched girl out of my mind. In a way, it's a kind of sickness.* He was glad of the Marquess's company. Peter was an old friend, a friend with whom he could always be on easy relaxed terms. Therefore, why could he not voice any of the turmoil that beset him when he thought of that wretched girl? Perhaps it would be a good idea to use Peter's visit to get away from the round of theatres, balls and routs.

Strange that Peter had never shown much interest in any woman, although they all ran after him as hard as they could. He was extremely handsome, as dark as Lord Sylvester was fair. He had thick, black hair, as black as Minerva's, thought Lord Sylvester with a sudden wrench at his heart. His eyes were a peculiar tawny shade, "sherry" eyes, and he had a strong face with a prominent domineering nose over a firm mouth and cleft chin. He had an easy, panther-like grace and danced superbly—as most of Wellington's officers did.

He suddenly realized that Peter was talking about Minerva again. "I kept hearing her name over and over again at White's the other evening," said the Marquess. "Bryce, Blenkinsop, Chumley and Dubois were all in a huddle, plotting something."

"Indeed! What, pray?"

"I don't know. I just caught her name mentioned over and over again and they seemed to be sniggering quite horribly. It was as if they had something quite dreadful planned for her. That Dubois is an evil man. He's the best shot in England and twice he's killed a man in a duel. He always gets the other fellow to call him out so that he can look innocent. Tell me about Miss Minerva Armitage."

"There's not much to tell," said Lord Sylvester, affecting a yawn. "She's a country vicar's daughter who is being brought out by Lady Godolphin . . ."

"Good heavens, that old rip."

"Exactly. That dreadful old lady and her malapropisms. Do you know she actually talked about the British troops storming the French fornications? Although sometimes I think she does it deliberately.

"She has her eye on Chumley as a mate for her charge and Miss Armitage's cousins are come to town and affected to take an interest in Chumley, merely, of course, to annoy Minerva. So Lady Godolphin descends on Miss Josephine Armitage, compliments her on her gown, and assures her, "You are looking quite vaginal, my love. Quite vaginal." Fortunately none of the Armitage girls had ever heard the word before and merely grasped that she meant "virginal" so the shaft fell wide. The cousins have money, and Miss Minerva has none, as they keep on pointing out."

"I am beginning to be overcome by a desire to meet this Minerva."

"Then we shall call. But she's an ordinary sort of girl. Nothing out of the common way. I find myself too often made sorry for her. She has to marry or her fox-hunting father will end in the River Tick.

"For some reason, the four you have mentioned are always underfoot, together with the unlikely combination of Barding, Yarwood and Fresne, so they do not give her much chance to fix her affections on anyone more suitable. It is my belief she'll settle for Chumley."

"Oh, she'll probably do very well," shrugged the Marquess. "Women are quite hard-headed when it comes to marriage. They're happier settling for money instead of love."

He spoke with a trace of bitterness in his voice and Lord Sylvester looked at him curiously. Before he inherited the marquessate, Peter had not had a feather to fly with. Had some girl rejected him in the past due to his lack of funds? It was no use asking. Peter would laugh and deny it.

He contented himself by saying, "We shall call on Miss Armitage this afternoon and you can satisfy your curiosity."

They were lucky to call at a time when Lady Godolphin was lying down and Minerva's usual court was absent.

The Marquess was taken aback by Minerva's unexpected beauty. Her skin was pale, almost luminous, and her black hair shone with purple lights. She treated them both courteously, seeming very poised and at ease. But the Marquess picked up the tension between the pair and wondered at it. His friend, Sylvester, seemed to be holding himself on a very tight rein and at last said abruptly, "So you still plan to marry Chumley?"

"I do not know," said Minerva. "I am to meet his parents. He says it is important to know someone's background before making any major decisions."

"As serious as that," said Lord Sylvester, raising his thin eyebrows. "Lady Godolphin must be in ecstasies. He has no doubt asked her permission to pay his addresses."

Minerva looked awkward and pleated a fold of her silk gown between nervous fingers.

"He asked me not to tell her. His parents are visiting relatives at a place near Barnet. Lord Chumley suggested I tell Lady Godolphin that I am going driving with him. He is being very thoughtful, You see, if we should not suit, and

{ 147 }

we come to that decision after I have met his family, then Lady Godolphin will not be so disappointed.''

''And when is this to take place?''

''Saturday.''

''This Saturday? And how are you to explain your absence for such a long time to Lady Godolphin? You will be gone several hours and that is an overlong time for a simple drive in the Park.''

''Lady Godolphin has accepted an invitation to the Aubryns' rout so she will not be here.''

''I think you should tell Lady Godolphin,'' said the Marquess suddenly, thinking of the sniggers and low voices he had heard in White's.

''Oh, no, I could not do that,'' said Minerva simply. ''I gave Lord Chumley my word. Perhaps I should not have told *you*. But he only said not to tell Lady Godolphin.''

''I do not think, after some reflection,'' said Lord Sylvester, ''that Lady Godolphin is a good chaperone for you. For example, much as we delight in your company, you should not be allowed to entertain two gentlemen without a duenna.''

Minerva gave a weary little shrug. She looked over at the two handsome men seated opposite her and wanted to explain to them that she had no choice. She had prayed and prayed and her duty was plain. She must marry quickly.

At that point, Josephine and Emily Armitage and their mother were announced and came in on a wave of silks and lace. Lady Edwin all but ignored Minerva, Josephine and Emily completely ignored Minerva, as all three set their sights on Lord Sylvester and the Marquess.

Peter, Marquess of Brabington, found he could not bear the atmosphere any longer and rose to his feet, saying they must take their leave.

Lady Edwin and her daughters promptly rose as well, remembering all sorts of engagements. The Marquess turned in the doorway, after ushering the others out, and tried to say something. Minerva sat very still and quiet, her hands folded in her lap. Instead he gave a curt little bow, followed the others, and quite rudely extricated Lord Sylvester from the ladies.

"Phew!" said the Marquess. "That poor, pretty little thing! Well, now I have met her and seen her predicament, I think there is only one course which lies open."

"Which is?" demanded Lord Sylvester curiously, as the two friends strolled arm in arm across Hanover Square.

"First of all, I assume you don't want to marry her yourself?"

There was a long silence. Then Lord Sylvester said in a low voice, "She is very young and innocent and country bred. It would not answer."

"Exactly," said the Marquess cheerfully. "So, the answer is this, you are rich and I am rich. We go to Hopeworth and give this wretched vicar enough money to pull him up by the bootstraps on condition he takes his daughter home."

"He might not take it," pointed out Lord Sylvester.

"Tell him it's a loan. Send that steward of yours to oversee his farms and land. You know, Dawson. Dawson could grow anything anywhere. The man's a wizard."

"Perhaps she wants to marry Chumley."

"Stuff! Nobody wants to marry Chumley, except perhaps his mother. And what's this about his parents visiting Barnet? His ma don't move from that barn of a place they've got in Sussex and pa does what ma says, so what are they doing in Barnet? In any case, to return to the vicar. We could see the prize fight on Saturday, call on the vicar, and enjoy ourselves at the same time."

"You go, Peter," said Lord Sylvester, stopping suddenly. "We'll arrange the money business between our lawyers, and I'll send for Dawson if the vicar's willing. I think this Barnet matter ought to be looked into."

"Of course."

"Why are you smiling like that?"

"Oh, nothing," said the Marquess hurriedly. "I must have been thinking of the prize fight."

Minerva, who had risen after their departure to watch them from the window, let the curtain drop with a sigh. But she had little things to comfort her, she thought drearily. The three Dandies had only called once, and then only to preen and strut in front of her, restored to their former glory. Their conversation had been barbed and malicious. Minerva knew they would not forgive her for tricking them.

Then, it appeared from his manner, that she need not worry about any further attentions from Lord Sylvester Comfrey. She had probably disgusted him by surrendering so easily to his embrace. It was as well she was guided by duty. She could now forget him and be easy in her conscience.

Lady Godolphin was socially acceptable but viewed as definitely not respectable by the mothers of hopeful debutantes. And so that was the reason Minerva did not have any female friends to confide in. Just any one ordinary debutante would have pointed out that Lady Godolphin should most certainly be told of her proposed expedition with Lord Chumley. A more respectable chaperone than Lady Godolphin would have made sure she at least took her maid along with her. But as it was, Minerva knew only enough about the conventions to find it quite suitable to travel alone with Lord Chumley, provided it was not in a closed carriage.

Nevertheless she could not help hoping it would rain, so that the visit could be postponed.

She was further depressed to receive a letter from Annabelle who mentioned that Guy Wentwater had returned, and although he had gone to visit relatives, she, Annabelle, intended to tell her parents of her determination to see the young man on his return.

What could have changed her mind? thought Minerva. Annabelle had seemed glad to escape from Guy Wentwater. Why should she encourage his advances now?

It was more than ever imperative that she, Minerva, should marry and be able to give Annabelle a Season.

The weather was quite dreadful for the rest of the week, unseasonably chilly and damp and very rainy.

Minerva visited the opera, the Royal Academy, two breakfasts and a rout, but Lord Sylvester was absent and

Lord Chumley was always dutifully at her side to fetch her refreshment and hold her fan.

Minerva often wondered what on earth they would find to talk about once they were married. Lord Chumley had very little conversation, and such that he did have centred around prize fights and cock fights and the latest wonder to be seen at Astley's Amphitheatre—the latter being a display of acrobatics by genuine English Bedouin, unlike the "ugly" foreigners who could been seen "waving their big ugly feet in the air like frying pans" at a rival establishment.

Infuriatingly, Saturday dawned clear and fair. They were to leave as early as ten o'clock, Lord Chumley had said, guessing correctly that Lady Godolphin would not be awake at that time.

She hesitated a little before allowing Lord Chumley to help her up onto the box of his carriage. She had thought there would be a groom, or at least a tiger, in attendance.

Perhaps Minerva might have refused to go. But just at that moment, she saw Lord Sylvester turning the corner of the square. She folded her lips into a thin line. He would see that she meant to carry things through to the bitter end.

Lord Chumley said little and drove fast. Minerva barely noticed where they were going. Misery seemed to clutch her heart. The very act of meeting his parents was to seal her doom. On through North London they sped and out into the countryside, easily passing other carriages and coaches on the road.

They seemed to have been travelling for a very long time when Lord Chumley suddenly swung off the main road, and the carriage bumped along a rutted lane, shadowed by overhanging trees. The horses slowed to a canter and all the quiet noises of the countryside crowded in; birds twittered from the hedgerows, a dog barked in the distance, and somewhere nearby, a cow lowed mournfully.

"Nearly there," said Lord Chumley with a tight little smile.

"At your parents?" demanded Minerva in surprise.

"Not yet," he replied. "Just going to get a fresh team put to."

"But there cannot possibly be a posting house on this lane," exclaimed Minerva.

"Best place there is," he said, urging the weary horses forward.

They swung around a bend and pulled up before a long, low hostelry. A weatherbeaten sign proclaimed it to be The Duke of Clarence—a grand name for what appeared to be little more than a hedge tavern.

Three horses were tethered outside, so Minerva decided it must be grander inside than out, since it seemed to attract custom.

"We'll have some refreshment," said Lord Chumley.

"Isn't there even an ostler?" Minerva looked down at Lord Chumley in surprise. His lordship had sprung down and seemed to be about to see to his horses himself.

"My love," he said sternly, "you must not ask so many questions. Let me assist you down. There! Now you will be able to partake of some refreshment."

He had tethered the horses and was leading her towards the inn.

How very quiet it was!

There was no sound from inside, not even the banging of a pewter pot or the clink of a glass.

She hesitated slightly. Lord Chumley held her arm in a surprisingly strong clasp. "Come along, my dear," he said. "One would think you were afraid."

Minerva reluctantly allowed him to lead her into the inn. Three men arose at her entrance and she stared in amazement.

There was Mr. Jeremy Bryce, looking more to one side than ever, Mr. Harry Blenkinsop, fat and florid, and Mr. Silas Dubois, his small, slight, almost crooked figure dominated by his large nose.

Minerva whirled around as the door slammed behind her.

Lord Chumley stood looking at her, swinging the large key in his hand. He no longer looked weak and foolish, but nasty and dangerous, and he seemed to have grown bigger in the dim light of the tap room.

''What is the meaning of this?'' demanded Minerva in a shaky voice.

Mr. Blenkinsop acted as spokesman. ''We think it's time you were schooled to behave like a real woman. So you've got to pick whichever one of us is going to deflower you. We're acting like gentlemen by giving you a choice.''

''You're mad!'' said Minerva. She turned on Lord Chumley. ''And I must have been mad to even consider marriage with you. You all disgust me . . . you *excuses* for manhood.''

''Very fine,'' sneered Harry Blenkinsop. ''Let me put it this way. You take one of us . . . or all.''

Minerva began to scream.

They simply watched her, making no effort to silence her.

''You can't be heard,'' said Mr. Bryce, picking his teeth. ''Ain't anybody about for miles.''

Minerva fought back an overwhelming desire to burst into tears.

''God help me,'' she said simply.

''There she goes again,'' sneered Silas Dubois. ''Always praying. Well, this is one time your prayers ain't going to be answered. We'll draw straws, boys, for who has her first.''

''I s-say,'' said Lord Chumley. ''The joke's gone far enough. We only meant to give you a little fright, Minerva. Now, I'' . . . here he struck his chest ''. . . I am willing to marry you!''

Minerva looked at him with infinite contempt.

''I would as soon be wed to a broken-down sheep,'' she said coldly, ''for that is exactly what you look like.''

The other three roared with malicious laughter and Lord Chumley turned as red as fire with rage.

''Let me at her,'' he said thickly.

''Easy. Steady,'' said Silas Dubois. ''We draw first.''

It's so *stupid*, thought Minerva wildly. She looked about for escape, for a weapon, *anything*.

''There's no way out,'' said Silas Dubois.

''Except by the window,'' came a mocking voice.

Minerva gave a cry of relief. The window had swung

{ 153 }

open and Lord Sylvester Comfrey stepped easily over the sill and onto the dirty floor of the tap room.

"Now who has the key?" he said pleasantly.

"Get him!" yelled Dubois. "There's four of us."

Lord Sylvester thrust Minerva into a corner and braced himself for the onslaught. Minerva buried her face in her hands.

There were cries and thuds and cracks and groans and scuffles and gasps and at long last a dead silence.

She uncovered her face.

Lord Sylvester was standing alone in the middle of the room.

Lord Chumley and Jeremy Bryce were knocked out cold. Harry Blenkinsop had his head stuffed up the chimney and Silas Dubois was crouched behind a settle, holding a handkerchief to his bloody nose.

"The key," said Lord Sylvester.

"Chumley has it," whispered Minerva, as if all her tormenters would spring to life if she spoke in too loud a voice.

Lord Sylvester stooped over the fallen body of Lord Chumley and extracted the key. One of his hands was bleeding at the knuckles, but, apart from that, he looked almost as if he were paying a morning call.

"Come along, Minerva," he said.

He put an arm around her and led her to the door.

"I wouldn't waste your time," came the sneering voice of Silas Dubois. "She's not any good once you get the skirts over her head. They're all the same."

Lord Sylvester walked forward quickly, raised his gloves and struck Silas Dubois full across the face.

"Name your second, Dubois," he said.

Mr. Dubois gave a slow, twisted smile. "Bryce shall act for me," he said.

"And Brabington shall act for me. Minerva, your arm. Let us leave these creatures."

Minerva leaned against him outside the inn, drinking in great gulps of fresh air.

"Don't speak," he said. He threw her up into his racing curricle, climbed up and took the reins. "We shall find a respectable inn at Barnet. Don't cry, Minerva. I have worries enough without a watering pot crying over my sleeve and shrinking the material."

But Minerva's nerves were quite overset and she cried and gulped and sobbed all the way to Barnet.

"You do look a mess," said his lordship, rolling into the yard of a well-kept inn. "Your nose is all red and your eyes are mere slits."

"You have no sensitivity whatsoever," said Minerva. But she took a steel mirror out of her reticule and looked in dismay at the wreck of her appearance. "How on earth did you find me?" she asked, pushing strands of hair under her bonnet.

"I followed you. It was all very simple."

Lord Sylvester arranged a room for her at the inn and sent her off with the landlord's wife to bathe her eyes.

After an half hour, she joined him in a private parlour, a speech of thanks and gratitude on her lips.

"No," he said, holding up a slender hand to forestall her. "I can see you are about to burst into a noble speech and I could not bear it. Sit down and drink your wine. It's of no use explaining. I never knew a female who embroils me in such a mess."

"You will not meet Dubois," said Minerva. "Duelling is illegal."

"So it is," he agreed, helping himself to wine. "But I most certainly shall meet him. It is a point of honour. Of course, I should not have fallen into the trap. Dubois is famous for promoting duels."

"He is supposed to be the best marksman in England," exclaimed Minerva. "And he will kill you! And all because of my stupidity."

"Now, don't cry again or I shall slap you. Silas will undoubtedly try to kill me. But if I am allowed peace and quiet to think, I may be able to outwit him."

"What shall I tell Lady Godolphin?"

"Tell her you went driving with me instead. If you tell her the truth, she will rage all over London and you may find your reputation in rags. Do not tell anyone about the duel. That, too, could ruin you. You have your family to think of.

In fact, Minerva, it's high time you went home. London and its evil ways are not for you.''

"But my family . . .''

"I have heard a rumour that your father has come into money. You will no doubt have a letter from him in the next few days, begging for your return. Think on't, Minerva. Peace and quiet, the parish rounds, the bucolic silence of Hopeworth.''

"I shall miss you. . . .''

"You will remember me sometimes when you are happily married, and you will wonder what ever came over you. You must not fancy yourself in love with me. It would not serve.''

"Why?'' asked Minerva in a low voice.

The sunlight shone in long shafts onto the sanded floor of the parlour. Golden dust motes floated between them. A burst of laughter came from the yard below and a horse snorted and stamped.

"I am too old for you, Minerva. You will change as you grow and the man you will want at twenty-five is not the man you want now. People change.''

"What if you die?''

"Then you may lay flowers on my grave. But I do not think I shall die.''

"When and where are you going to meet Dubois?''

"I shall leave that to Brabington. One's second arranges things like that.''

"Let me know.''

"Why, Minerva? So that you can call the Runners?''

"So that I can pray for you.''

"In that case, perhaps . . . let us talk of other things.''

He talked away lightly while Minerva sat listening to him, watching his face, watching his hands, wondering if she would ever love anyone else. For she knew at last that she was totally and completely in love with him. Somehow, she forced herself to smile and talk easily. The journey back from Barnet seemed so short. There was no chance of a private goodbye, for Lady Godolphin arrived in her carriage at the same time, demanding explanations as to why Minerva was not with Chumley.

At last, Lord Sylvester drove off and Minerva sadly watched him go, and Lady Godolphin had to tug at her arm to bring her to her senses.

Chapter Eleven

"Well, when is it to be? Since I don't suppose Dubois has any intention of giving up a chance of putting a ball in my heart. He's always hated me, but since the advent of Minerva, it's grown to a madness."

The Marquess of Brabington nodded. "He's desperate to meet you. Chalk Farm. Wednesday morning at six."

"I'll be there."

"He'll kill you."

"Perhaps. Perhaps not. I have a trick or two up my sleeve. I am pleased the good vicar accepted our generosity. Good works suit you, Peter. There has been a glow in your eyes since you returned."

The Marquess shrugged. "They are a pleasant family. I enjoyed the prize fight and my subsequent visit to Hopeworth. It is a fine thing to play Lord Bountiful, particularly as Mr. Armitage had absolutely no qualms about accepting our bounty. As I recall, he compared himself to Elijah the Tishbite and me to a friendly raven who brought him bread and flesh in the morning and bread and fish in the evening. It was quite uplifting. He was also delighted at the thought of having his eldest daughter back in the bosom of the family. It appears she rules the roost. Charming family."

"A little young for you," said Lord Sylvester, lifting down a heavy wooden box.

"I don't know what on earth you are talking about," said the Marquess acidly. "Oh, I say, what have you there?"

"Engines of death," said Lord Sylvester, throwing back the lid.

The Marquess whistled in awe. "They're beauties. Where on earth did you get pistols like these?"

"My secret. I had them especially made last year when it seemed as if some young hothead intended to blow my brains out. But he cooled in time and I've never had to use them."

They were undoubtedly duelling pistols as opposed to military pistols. They were long and dull and deadly.

Here was no fancy scrollwork or embellishment to supply a target. The interior of the barrel was highly polished but the outside was browned to reduce glare to the duellist's eye when the pistol came into the aim.

The inside of the barrel was not rifled, for this was considered unsporting, since rifling increased the speed of the bullet.

They were flintlocks and the wooden butts were "checked" —scored in a criss-cross fashion to give the perfect grip. What was unusual about these pistols was their "saw handle grip." The wood of the stock was shaped so that there was a protuberance that fitted over the thumb web of the firer's hand. The Marquess reverently lifted one out. It fitted so sleekly into his hand that all he had to do was point, and the gun automatically pointed exactly at the spot that the firer's brain and eye would be aiming at.

The idea of the duelling pistol was that it should have this "pointing" ability.

With Lord Sylvester's innovation to the butt or grip, his weapons became literally an extension of the arm, and missing the target was well-nigh impossible.

Of course, thought the Marquess with a sudden shiver, Sylvester, as the challenger, had the right to offer his own choice of pistol, so this would mean Dubois would be using one of them and would also be unable to miss.

He carefully laid it back in the box.

"Be careful," said Lord Sylvester with a crooked grin. "I've had them especially fitted with springs so light that they are hairtriggers. The slightest touch on the trigger will discharge it."

"It's terrible," said the Marquess. "When I raised it, the balance was so superb that the damn thing seemed like a part of my arm. One of these in Silas Dubois' hands will be the end of you."

"I have a plan," said Lord Sylvester, "which may work. On the other hand, I might be killed. Do you think Minerva will weep for me, Peter? Or will she shortly lie in the marital arms of some bucolic country squire?"

"Does it matter?" asked the Marquess sharply.

"Of course it matters," laughed his friend. "I am fighting over her honour, remember? I would like to think she would cry for me."

"She will," said the Marquess. "She's in love with you."

For a moment some intense emotion gleamed in Lord Sylvester's green eyes, and then he sighed. "She is too young, Peter, to know what love is. Let us hope I live to think of her from time to time as a pretty memory."

"You will not be going to the Aubryns' masked ball on Tuesday night?" asked the Marquess.

"No. I shall stay at home and commune with my soul. If you are there, Peter, see that my fair Minerva is not plagued by unwelcome suitors."

When the Marquess first saw Minerva at the Aubryns' ball, he was overcome with a strong desire to shake her until her teeth rattled.

She had no right to look so carefree or so beautiful.

Minerva was dressed as Minerva. She wore a gold helmet and a filmy white Roman gown and gold Roman sandals. She carried a gold staff topped with a golden owl.

She was not wearing a mask, and he found himself thinking more kindly of her when he noticed the anguish in her wide eyes.

"Where is he?" were the first words she asked.

"Sylvester? Having a quiet evening at home," replied the

Marquess easily. "Now, perhaps I could fetch you some refreshment, Miss Armitage?"

"No. I mean, yes. Come with me where we can talk,"
said Minerva wildly.

They sat down in a corner of the refreshment room. "The
duel must be tomorrow," said Minerva. "I know it's tomorrow. It's all my fault. If he dies I will kill myself."

"You must think of your family," said the Marquess severely. "I saw them the other day, but no doubt you know
about that."

"No," said Minerva. "Why should you visit my family?"

The Marquess hesitated, and then made up his mind. Minerva should know of Sylvester's generosity.

He explained about the money and the steward and that
the vicar would shortly be sending for his eldest daughter.

"Oh! Oh! Oh!" cried Minerva, her hands flying to her
pale cheeks. "This is terrible. He is so good, so kind, so
generous. I had thought him a heartless rake. And I am
sending him to his death."

"Calm yourself," urged the Marquess. "It is highly unlikely that Sylvester will die."

Minerva looked at him, suddenly as calm as she had been
agitated a moment before.

"Please, could you fetch me some champagne, my
lord," she asked, not looking at him.

"Certainly," said the Marquess coldly, immediately putting all her concern down to frivolous, feminine hysterics.

But when he returned with the champagne, Minerva had
gone. He diligently searched the ballroom, but could find no
sign of her.

At last he ran Lady Godolphin to earth.

"I don't know what's come over her these past days.
She's getting more and more notorious."

The Marquess looked at her in a puzzled way, and then
remembered her ladyship's malapropisms and gathered that
she had meant "nervous."

"Perhaps she's gone home," suggested Lady Godolphin.
"Ask if my carriage has been called for."

This the Marquess did. He found that Minerva had indeed

called for the Godolphin carriage. He shrugged. At least he could turn his attention to the other pretty girls and forget about Minerva . . . and forget about an enchanting face with two blue eyes, framed in a cloud of blonde hair which had haunted him since he had left Hopeworth.

Minerva sat grimly in Lady Godolphin's carriage as it rumbled through the night streets. By the time Lady Godolphin found out where her charge had gone, it would be morning. Colonel Brian had been at the ball which meant that Lady Godolphin would stay until dawn.

In the flickering light of the parish lamps, Minerva's face was white and set. Her mind was made up. He probably would not stay alive to marry her even if he wanted to. And so she would spend this last night with him.

The carriage rolled to a stop outside Lord Sylvester's house in St. James's Square.

The footmen jumped from the backstrap and let down the steps. The coachman craned his head.

"There don't look like no rout a-going on here, miss," he called down from the box. "Would you like us to wait?"

"No, John," said Minerva. "I am quite all right. Please go."

She mounted the shallow steps and then turned, waiting for the coach to drive away. When it had turned the corner of the square, she took a deep breath and seized the knocker.

A rather evil-looking butler answered the door, bringing to Minerva's mind tales that Lord Sylvester hired his servants from the gutter.

"I am Miss Armitage," she said firmly, "come to call on his lordship."

The butler peered past her at the deserted square and then held a branch of candles higher to take a better look at the vision confronting him. His eyes travelled from her golden helmet to her golden sandals and then to the staff with the owl on top which she still carried in one hand.

"See here, miss," he said placatingly. "You'd better let me fetch you a hack. His lordship is not at home."

Minerva leaned weakly against the doorjamb. "Not at home?" she echoed.

"Hey there! Bustle about! Fetch another bottle," shouted a familiar voice.

"Sylvester!" cried Minerva. Before the butler had time to block her way, she had nipped past him. She threw open the door of a study off the hall and stood poised on the threshold.

Lord Sylvester was sitting in a wing chair beside the fire with an empty brandy bottle on the table in front of him.

He stared at Minerva and passed his hand over his eyes and stared again.

"She would push past me, me lord," came the querulous voice of his butler. "I told her you wasn't home."

"That's all right," said Lord Sylvester vaguely. "Bring another bottle and another glass and leave us."

Minerva walked forward and stood looking down at him.

"Well, my wise goddess," said Lord Sylvester, "as you can see I am quite drunk. What is your pleasure, Miss Armitage?"

"You," answered Minerva, through white lips. "You, my lord."

"I'm not drunk. *You* are. Do sit down, Minerva, and stop looking heroic. I can't bear you when you're noble."

A servant entered with another bottle of brandy and a glass for Minerva.

"Now," said Lord Sylvester, when they were alone again, "I suppose you have winkled the intelligence out of Peter that I fight this duel in the morning and that you have felt yourself responsible for my imminent death and so have come to sacrifice your fair body. Go home, Minerva. I do not seduce virgins. Very boring things, virgins."

"Do you intend to drink that stuff all by yourself?" said Minerva coldly. "Or am I allowed to have some?"

"By all means." He poured her a glass and his glittering drink-fevered eyes watched in amazement as she downed it in one gulp.

"Well, answer me," he said harshly. "You came to sacrifice yourself on the altar of my dissolute body, did you not?"

"Yes," said Minerva, filling up her glass again, and disposing of it as quickly as the last. The brandy was giving her a reckless, heady feeling and she no longer felt afraid.

She looked at him steadily. He was not wearing a coat and was attired only in a thin cambric shirt, open at the neck, leather breeches and hessian boots. Apart from the glitter in his green eyes, he seemed quite sober.

"Go away, Minerva," he sighed. "The thought of bedding a noble gesture makes me go cold all over. If you leave now, no one will know you have been here."

"Except Lady Godolphin's servants," said Minerva calmly.

"I shall bribe 'em."

"No, I think you have spent enough money on the Armitage family. The Marquess of Brabington told me of your kindness, your generosity . . ."

"It's his generosity as well," interrupted Lord Sylvester rudely. "Anyway, I only did it to be rid of you, Minerva. Go home."

"No."

"My love, I am very drunk. I am shortly about to retire so that I may have a clear and sober head in the morning. I fear I may have misled you by my attentions. I am an incorrigible flirt. I have no interest in you whatsoever. I do not find you attractive. You bore me. There. Have I made myself plain?"

"Yes," said Minerva, her eyes filling with tears. "You have made yourself very plain. I will leave you now, my lord. Despite your cruel remarks, I wish you good fortune tomorrow. Oh, I wish to God I had never set eyes on you."

"There, now," he said. "I was too harsh. Come and kiss me goodbye, Minerva, and I will take you home."

The room was lit only by the flickering firelight. The furniture and pictures seemed to dance and waver in the reflections of the flames.

Minerva rose wearily and went over and placed a cold kiss on his cheek.

All at once he could smell that light flower perfume she wore and he could feel the heavy weight of one of her breasts against his arm, and very gently he put up a hand and buried it in the back tresses of her hair which cascaded from under the gold helmet. He increased the pressure, brought up his other hand and pulled her down onto his lap. The helmet went tumbling to the floor.

All at once, he was kissing her quite desperately, lost in a hot magic world of lips and breasts and shining hair. He tried to control himself, to pull back, but one timid little hand crept inside his shirt and he thought he would die if he did not have her.

If she had cried out, or protested, he would have come to his senses immediately, but she seemed a thing of passion, a throbbing, pulsating, burning woman.

Even when she was tumbled, naked, under him on the floor, and a voice in his head was crying out she was a virgin, she ran her nails down his back in such a way that all hell broke loose and he could not stop until he was twisting and turning and dying inside her.

And even when he gently pulled her clothes on again, it was to gather her closely in his arms against his breast and carry her upstairs to his bed so that he could rediscover the wealth and wonder he had just found.

"Perhaps he will not come," said Silas Dubois, biting his nails.

"Damn you," said the Marquess of Brabington. "Don't suspect Lord Sylvester of your own low, twisted values. He will come."

A thin ground mist was turning gold as the sun rose above the church tower. The clock chimed six and a skylark started up as if surprised by the noise.

The Marquess found himself suffering a revulsion against the whole of London society which tolerated such awful toads as Dubois and his second, Jeremy Bryce. The surgeon, Mr. Mackintosh, approached and asked in a low voice if everything had been done to try to bring the duel to an end.

"Of course it has," said the Marquess harshly. "I do not enjoy the spectacle of my best friend putting his life at risk."

"I think I hear his lordship now," said the surgeon. The steady clop of horses' hooves sounded in the distance.

"Whoever it is, he's not in too great a hurry," sneered Silas Dubois.

Driving his racing curricle, Lord Sylvester drove onto the field.

"The fool!" muttered Silas Dubois.

He himself was dressed from head to foot in black. Even the buttons of his coat had been painted black so as to offer no target to his antagonist.

Lord Sylvester on the other hand was dressed in a Spanish blue coat with silver buttons worn over a striped Marseilles waistcoat and a ruffled shirt and starched cravat. A pair of buff breeches and suwarrow boots completed the ensemble. His lordship raised his quizzing glass and surveyed Mr. Dubois before letting it fall.

The surgeon removed his black hat and leaned on his gold-topped cane as if Lord Sylvester were already dead.

"Let's not waste any time," said Lord Sylvester languidly. "Choose your weapon, Dubois."

Silas squinted into the box and let out a low whistle. He lifted one out, and leered up at Lord Sylvester. "Your determination to play the gentleman, Comfrey, is suicidal."

"Be careful," said Lord Sylvester. "They have hairtriggers."

Never had Lord Sylvester looked so calm or so indolent. Never before had his mind worked so furiously.

The pistols were primed and loaded and the instructions given. They were to stand back to back, count to ten, turn and fire immediately. To withhold their fire, hoping the other would miss or wound slightly, then calmly take aim to kill was unsporting, and the one who did that would be disgraced.

The morning suddenly seemed very still and quiet. This is it! thought Lord Sylvester, his thoughts tumbling one after the other. "I never said I loved her. I should have asked her to marry me. I must not die!" And then his brain became calm again.

The pistols were cocked and he stood back to back with Silas Dubois.

Now, it is instinctive to start on the left foot because the pistol is held high in the right hand. But starting on the left foot means ending the tenth pace on the right foot, which means a vital second or two lost while the duellist brings his left foot up to his right one in order to turn around. By starting off on his right foot, Lord Sylvester planned to end his tenth pace on his left with the right foot behind him so that he would simply have to swivel round to be facing Dubois.

As he walked his paces, Lord Sylvester slowly brought his pistol arm down. The Marquess held his breath and wondered what his friend was doing. The normal way of duelling was to hold the pistol high, turn, and then bring the pistol down and forward into the aim. While this is happening, however, the opponent is obscured and cannot be fired at until the gun is levelled.

What Lord Sylvester planned to do was to bring the gun up from a down position so that Dubois would be in full view all the time, so that his actions could be seen, and so that Lord Sylvester could have a choice of aiming his pistol before Dubois' gun came to bear on him.

At the count of ten, Lord Sylvester swung around, his gun already coming up fast. He saw immediately that Dubois had also started on the right foot and was already facing him.

For a brief second, Silas Dubois' pistol obscured his vision as it came down to "point," but Lord Sylvester, unable to beat Dubois at the turn, found he could beat him at the point. His pistol flashed up and he fired before Dubois could get his gun down.

Lord Sylvester's bullet hit precisely the spot he had aimed at . . . the barrel of Dubois' pistol.

The blow set off the hairtrigger and Dubois' gun discharged harmlessly into the air. The gun flew from Dubois' hand and he let out an almost animal scream of pain. His fingers had been broken.

Lord Sylvester calmly handed over his pistol to his second, the Marquess of Brabington. Jeremy Bryce and the surgeon, Mr. Mackintosh, hurried over to where the wounded Dubois was crouched on the ground, moaning faintly.

Mr. Mackintosh shook his head over the ruin of Dubois' hand. "Ye'll never duel again, Mr. Dubois," he said.

"When your trigger finger heals, I doubt if it will set properly. Ye'll never pull a trigger again."

Silas Dubois crouched, shaking, humiliated beyond belief. The story would be all over London by the end of the day. His faithless friend, Jeremy Bryce, would see to that. Already Bryce was trying to fawn on Lord Sylvester, praising his marksmanship.

The Marquess retrieved Silas Dubois' gun and brought it back to Lord Sylvester who examined it and shook his head sadly. It was ruined. He put the gun with his own in the case and looked around him.

How splendid it was to be alive and in love! Everything seemed fresh and new-minted.

Oblivious of the listening Dubois and Bryce and the surgeon, he clapped the Marquess on the shoulder. "We'll go and have a double celebration, Peter. I am to be wed. If she'll have me."

The Marquess grinned. He did not have to ask who the "she" was.

They strolled off, arm in arm.

The surgeon helped Silas Dubois to his feet and after setting his hand, adjusted a sling around his thin shoulders. "I have not done yet," muttered Silas Dubois.

"Heh, what?" exclaimed Jeremy Bryce. "Of course you're finished. The man made an absolute fool of you. But by George you were outclassed."

"By a trick," hissed Dubois. His eyes suddenly lit up with malice. "But I think I still have him. Hurry man. We must get to White's."

"At this hour?"

"Yes, at this hour. Hurry!"

Mr. Bryce kept silent on the road back to town, although he privately thought the shock must have addled his friend's wits.

Silas Dubois was muttering and biting the nails of his uninjured hand as the coach lurched and swayed. He barely waited for the steps to be let down when they at last reached St. James's Street, but leapt down and scuttled into the club and immediately started shouting for the betting book.

He took it over to a quiet corner and slowly turned the

pages. Ah, he had it! The entry seemed to leap out at him. "Mr. F, Sir Y and Lord B do hereby wager 50,000 pounds to be paid to the one who succeeds in winning the *prize* of Miss A's *affections*."

He scuttled over to a desk in the corner, and, producing a penknife from his pocket, he carefully cut out the page with the entry. He sharpened a quill and carefully changed the Lord B to Lord S. Then he wrote a brief letter and folded it, together with the page from the betting book, and sealed it and sent it to Minerva by one of the club servants.

Minerva was pacing up and down the Green Saloon in Lady Godolphin's home in Hanover Square, desperately waiting for news. Lady Godolphin was in bed and likely to remain there until noon at least, and Minerva did not know if her ladyship had found out about the visit to St. James's Square.

All Minerva's high standards had crumbled. Only let him live, she thought, and I will gladly become his mistress if he does not wish to marry me.

The sun climbed higher in the sky. He had kissed her passionately before sending her home in one of his carriages. She had stayed on his doorstep to watch him leave before departing herself, wondering if she would ever see him again.

The early morning post arrived with a letter from the vicar, telling of the generosity of Lord Sylvester and the Marquess of Brabington, and urging his daughter to come home.

And then Mice, the butler, was standing in the doorway announcing, "The Marquess of Brabington."

Minerva turned chalk white. Something must have happened or he would not have sent his second. Also, although he was holding it quite well, it was plain to see that the Marquess was very drunk.

"Servant, Miss Armitage," he said, making a very low bow and stumbling slightly as he did so.

"Sylvester!" cried Minerva. "Oh, tell me the worst. Don't keep me waiting in this agony."

"He is well, ma'am, and sends his respects."

"Wounded?"

"Goo' grashus, no. Fid as a fittle, I assure you. Shot the gun out o' Dubois' hand. Marvelush, 'slutely marvelush."

"Where is he at present?"

"Dead to the world. Dead drunk, that is."

"Oh," said Minerva in a small voice.

"There was somethin' else I was to say, but I'm bleshed if I can 'member. Good day to you."

"Wait!" screamed Minerva as the Marquess lurched to the door. "Did he not give any other message?"

"I'm sure he did, ma'am," said the Marquess swaying like a Lombardy poplar in a chopping wind. "But I can't 'member for the life of me."

And with that, he lurched out.

Minerva sat down very suddenly and stared at the floor.

He was safe.

And that was all right.

Fear clutched her heart. What had seemed like the love of a lifetime, a passionate noble giving of herself, now began to assume a sordid tinge.

What if he did not love her? What if she were pregnant? But he must love her. He had not said so, but his body and hands and mouth had. Her face began to burn.

But he should have called. Not sent his friend.

The butler appeared again and handed her a long sealed letter.

She broke the seal and crackled open the parchment. At first she could not really take in the contents. There was clearly the page out of a betting book. She stared at it in a puzzled way and then turned her attention to the accompanying letter.

"Dear Miss Armitage," she read. *"You may think Lord Sylvester Comfrey enamoured of you, but as you will see from the page which I took the Liberty of extracting from White's Betting Book, you have been made the subject of a Vulgar Wager.*
        "Be on your guard!
                Yr Humble & Obedient Servant,
                A Friend."

Minerva looked slowly at the page of the betting book again. This time, the item at the bottom of the page seemed to leap out at her. "Mr. F, Sir Y and Lord S do hereby wager 50,000 pounds to be paid to the one who succeeds in winning the *prize* of Miss A's *affections*," she read.

She let the papers fall to her lap. Now Lord Sylvester's generosity to her father seemed suspect. It would seem he had gone to great lengths to secure his prize.

But I gave myself to *him,* she told herself fiercely.

She shivered, feeling soiled and stupid and alone.

Someone knew about it. She had been made the subject of a wager, laughed about in the clubs.

All at once, she realized she had to get away, get back to Hopeworth. She did not want to see Lady Godolphin. Lady Godolphin was very much part of this hateful world.

There was only one letter she meant to write before she left.

Minerva arose and set about her business like a martinet. She packed only one small trunk. Fortunately, she had enough pin money left to pay for her travel.

She got a hack to the City, and from the City, the stage coach to Hopeminster, her slender resources only allowing her a place on the roof.

At Hopeminster, the landlord of the Cock and Feathers gladly agreed to supply miss with a chaise to take her to Hopeworth, saying her father would pay her shot on his next visit.

The day was dreary with a fine grey drizzle falling mournfully over the fields. Candles were being lit in the cottage windows as Minerva finally saw the squat tower of her father's church.

The fatigue of the two day long journey had served to calm her. She decided to tell her father that she had been so delighted to get his letter that she had left on the spot. Fortunately, during her short stay in London, she had spent most of her pin money shopping for presents for her family rather than buying things for herself, and these presents made up the major part of her luggage, and would make it seem more like a planned departure.

Her mood swung from rage where she dreamed of confronting Lord Sylvester and throwing the sheet of the betting book in his face, and bitter sadness when she thought she would be pregnant and have no future other than the bottom of the River Blyne.

When she thought of the Marquess's drunken state it all seemed part and parcel of that brutal world of men. Cock fighting, prize fights, and deflowering virgins, all a sport.

And to add to her burden of misery, her love and longing for him would not cease.

Perhaps she had never really known her father—always thinking of him as a bluff huntsman devoid of finer feelings.

But when the greetings were over and the presents exclaimed over and she had been hugged and fêted and questioned by her brothers and sisters, it was the vicar who had led her off to the study, it was her father who had shut the door and had wordlessly held out his pudgy arms, folding her in a tight embrace, letting her cry, and not asking one single question.

Chapter Twelve

The harvest was in and the chill winds of October swept across the brown fields. Red and gold leaves danced before the wind, branches tossed their arms up to the blustery sky where ragged clouds trailed curtains of rain over the county of Berham.

The whole countryside seemed in motion, and the vicar, from his sacrilegious perch on top of a table tombstone, could see Minerva's scarlet cloak billowing about her as she walked towards the village.

Bit by bit, the vicar had coaxed the tale of Minerva's indiscretion from her. He was at a loss as to what to do. In ordinary circumstances, he would have headed for London with his rifle primed and would have forced Lord Sylvester Comfrey to marry the girl.

But he was heavily indebted to Lord Sylvester for saving the family finances, and, furthermore, Minerva had made it quite plain that his lordship had been drunk and that she had thrown herself at him.

But he was at a loss to understand Lord Sylvester's behaviour. The vicar prided himself on being a good judge of character and he could have sworn Lord Sylvester was not the man to bed with any girl of gentle birth unless he had marriage in mind.

He had not confided in anyone for he felt Minerva's disgrace very deeply. But it made him ache to see her grow daily more spinsterish and withdrawn . . . She was not with child, thank the good Lord, but on a fair way to blighting her looks and her youth.

It was of no use unburdening himself to his wife, for Mrs. Armitage would be guaranteed to have quite a dreadful Spasm. He worried the problem of the betting book over and over in his head like one of his hounds worrying a bone. He knew such bets were made. He had made similar bets himself, but in a sort of lighthearted way, and the female concerned had never learned of them.

It was unlikely that someone of Lord Sylvester's calibre would make such a bet with a couple of mushrooms like Sir Peter Yarwood and Hugh Fresne.

But his lordship's very silence damned him. If his intentions towards Minerva had been at all honourable then he would surely have at least written.

All at once the problem seemed too heavy for one man. The vicar knew he would never enjoy the hunting season with such a burden on his mind. He decided to break his silence and visit Squire Radford.

The squire's very presence was soothing thought the vicar, when, a few hours later he was sitting by the fire in the squire's house; sipping the squire's excellent port. The squire sat in an armchair facing him, his feet in their buckled shoes scarcely touching the floor.

"Annabelle again?" asked the squire, after studying his friend for some moments.

"No," said the vicar. "It's worse than that. Much worse. It's Minerva."

There was another long silence, broken only by the sonorous ticking of a grandfather clock in the corner.

"Minerva left London very suddenly," ventured the squire.

"I got this here letter from Lady Godolphin," grumbled the vicar, pulling a crumpled paper from his pocket. "She's still going on about resuscitation."

The squire raised his eyebrows, and then smiled. "I suppose her ladyship means "restitution" or more likely "remuneration." In short, she wants her money back."

"And o'course she'll have it but it does seem a great plaguey amount for a few gowns," said the vicar, returning the letter to one of his capacious pockets.

"But that is not really what is troubling you," prompted the squire gently.

"Well, no. See, Jimmy, it's like this . . ." And the much embarrassed vicar plunged into a long tale of Minerva's fall from grace.

The squire listened patiently without interrupting once. At last the vicar finished and leaned back in his chair and mopped his brow with a handkerchief, looking hopefully at the squire for consolation or advice.

Squire Radford successfully hid his shock. He privately thought Minerva was a very lucky girl to still have a home, and that she had not been whipped and turned out of doors. But he was not a man to speak hastily and, after some reflection, he remembered all the girls of his youth who had fallen from virginity before they even reached the altar, but somehow everything had been hushed up and it had all seemed to work out in the end.

He turned over all he had heard about Lord Sylvester Comfrey in his mind. There was nothing he could remember which could explain his lordship's vulgar bet and subsequent behaviour.

In fact the more he thought about it, the more it seemed to him that Lord Sylvester had been very deeply in love with Minerva. His generosity to the vicar was solely so that Minerva should be able to return home since she was not happy in London.

"Lord Sylvester would not make any wager with such as Fresne and Yarwood," he said. "If it had been Lord Barding, I could have understood it. And this was sent to Minerva anonymously? Mmm. Do you have it with you?"

The vicar slapped at his capacious pockets and eventually found the page in a pocket in his tails.

The Squire searched among the clutter on the table next to his chair until he found a powerful magnifying glass. He studied the page carefully and then let out a sigh of satisfaction. "It was not Lord S," he said. "Someone altered it very cleverly. I think you will find it was originally Lord B."

"Here! Let me see!" cried the vicar. He screwed up his small eyes and peered through the glass at the paper. "Dashed if you ain't right, Jimmy! What a coil. But it still don't explain Sylvester's conduct. It explains Minerva's."

The Squire sank back in his chair and put the tips of his fingers together. There was a long silence. The clock ticked, the wind rattled the windows, and a log shifted and fell in the fire.

He thought about Minerva, and then about the two Minervas, the one rigidly held in, prim and proper, and the other, a wilful passionate woman who occasionally took over.

But Minerva was a woman and women, even intelligent ones, were apt to do the same stupid things given a certain set of circumstances.

He raised a gnarled finger and looked solemnly at the vicar.

"I think you will find that there is one thing Minerva did not tell you. . . ."

"And that is?" prompted the vicar.

"That she wrote Lord Sylvester a letter. She was hurt and furious, you must remember. Tell me Charles, when did any hurt and furious woman *not* write a letter?"

"But she would have told me . . ."

"Not necessarily. Not if it was a really nasty letter that she was secretly ashamed of writing."

"Surely . . ."

"Even genteel women can be very coarse when they are hurt. Take my word for it, Miss Minerva probably said some quite shocking things."

"Then all I have to do is tell her I know about it and get her to write and say she's sorry."

"No, she may still deny it. Womanlike, she may privately think he should have ignored it if he really loved her."

"Well, bless me, what can I do?"

The squire gave an impish smile. "We, my dear Charles,

will put our old heads together and write Lord Sylvester a letter—signed Minerva, of course—which will bring him panting down to Hopeworth.''

"What if he doesn't love her?''

"Oh, I think he does. We have nothing to lose. You see, if we persuade Minerva to write a letter and Lord Sylvester does not reply, then she will be more hurt than ever. This way is much better.''

"I don't know if I can write all that sentimental twaddle,'' said the vicar testily.

"Ah, we shall broach another bottle, Charles, and dream of our youth, and then you shall see. . . .''

Lord Sylvester Comfrey had been in London for the Little Season and was thankfully preparing to leave for the country. He was taking the Marquess of Brabington with him.

The Marquess had been on the point of rejoining his regiment in the Peninsula, but before he could set sail he was struck down with a violent fever, and had only just recovered.

He found the delights of London as dull as Lord Sylvester had found them and the one was as anxious as the other to shake the dust of the city from his heels.

The Marquess sometimes thought that Sylvester looked more like a man who had endured a grave illness than he did himself. Lord Sylvester had been curt and withdrawn ever since Minerva had left London. The Marquess knew she had sent his friend a letter and that the contents of that letter must have been quite dreadful to judge by the stricken look in Lord Sylvester's eyes.

Lord Sylvester had asked the Marquess what he had said to Minerva, whether he had told her of his, Lord Sylvester's love, and the Marquess had said guiltily that he could not remember a single thing about his visit.

Lord Sylvester himself had celebrated so freely and wildly after his duel that he had fallen asleep after sending the Marquess on his mission, not wanting to appear before his beloved in such a drunken state. He had not awoken until much later in the day and by that time Minerva's letter had been awaiting him.

She had said he disgusted her, that the very thought of what she had done with him nauseated her, and she never wanted to see or hear from him again.

Blind fury at her had carried him through the first weeks before cold hurt and misery had set in.

He had behaved very badly during the Little Season. He had been rude and haughty and had snubbed nearly the whole of London society. And how they had loved him for it! Lord Sylvester was every inch an aristocrat, a man of the *ton*.

He was weary of life and weary of himself.

His man announced that his travelling carriage had been brought around to the door.

"Come along, Peter," he smiled. "I can promise you some good shooting and fishing, and the air of the country will set you up no end."

Lord Sylvester wrapped himself in his many-caped benjamin and climbed onto the box of his travelling coach.

"You may drive, Peter," he said. "I have a deal of correspondence here."

The Marquess nodded and picked up the reins.

They were edging their way through the press of traffic in the Strand, when Lord Sylvester clutched his friend's arm, and cried, "Hopeworth, Peter! At all speed. She loves me!"

The Marquess glanced down at the parchment in Lord Sylvester's hand.

He suddenly felt better than he had done in months.

He had a vision of blonde hair and blue eyes and a bewitching smile.

"Hopeworth it is!" he grinned.

Lord Sylvester would have pressed on during the night, but the Marquess persuaded him to rack up for the night so that they could be dressed in their best when they presented themselves at the vicarage.

Lord Sylvester sat by the inn fire, reading his precious letter over and over again. The Marquess was only allowed a glimpse of it. It was written in a strangely old-fashioned spidery hand with all the s letters appearing as f.

"It obviously leaves you in no doubt of her affections, Sylvester," he said.

"Not a bit," smiled his friend. "The dear girl! Only see where her tears have blotted the page."

The squire had considered that bit a stroke of genius as he had sprinkled a few drops of water on the paper before sending it.

They were up early in the morning and soon setting a fast pace for Hopeworth.

The vicar was in his study when the two men called. The Marquess, who had already met the family, was disappointed to learn that Annabelle was at Lady Wentwater's but elected to sit and amuse Mrs. Armitage and the rest of the family while Lord Sylvester went to see the vicar.

The vicar cheerfully gave Lord Sylvester his permission to pay his addresses to Minerva.

"Wrote you a letter, heh?" said the vicar. "And she never said a word about it to me. Well, if you will take an older man's advice, my lord, I wouldn't mention that here letter. Much more diplomatic to say you came on your own without any inducement. Let's just put it on the fire."

"But it is a marvellous letter! A wonderful letter! No, no, my dear sir. I will not mention it, but I certainly mean to keep it among my dearest treasures."

The vicar sighed but did not press the point. He told Lord Sylvester about the betting book and how Minerva had been tricked, and then sent his lordship off to find her. "Minerva should by now be walking home from the village," he said.

Minerva was walking slowly along the narrow lane which led from the village of Hopeworth to the vicarage. Her heart had felt heavy since her father had told her how someone had tricked her by altering one letter in the betting book. She remembered every word of that horrible letter she had written and knew that with it she had effectively slammed the door in Lord Sylvester's face. No man would forgive her for a letter like that.

Her back ached from weariness. She had been assiduous in her parish duties, doing more work than she should. But it seemed infinitely preferable to fall into an exhausted sleep at night than to lie awake dreaming of a pair of green eyes and a beautifully sculptured mouth.

The day was very still, the sky above leaden, and unmelted frost glittered on the grass and sparkled on the bare branches of the tall hedges on either side of the road.

Her father had certainly consoled her by pointing out that her visit to London had prompted Lord Sylvester's generosity, and, thanks to his lordship and the Marquess of Brabington, the twins were now comfortably established in the King's Road, London, cramming for their entrance exams to Eton.

Ice crackled under the hard ring on the soles of her pattens. Winter was already settling down on the countryside. London, Lady Godolphin, her seven courtiers, the parties, the balls and the routs seemed at times as if they had never existed. Only Lord Sylvester remained real. Try as she would to forget him, she found she could remember every word he had said, every caress.

Perhaps she might see him again one day. His friend, the Marquess of Brabington, had seemed attracted to Annabelle when he had called to tell Papa that they need not worry about money any more. But he had not called again, so perhaps he had considered Annabelle too young. But for a while she had nourished dreams that Annabelle would marry the Marquess and somehow that way she would see Lord Sylvester again, if only at her sister's wedding.

She gave a little sigh and hitched her heavy work basket higher up on her arm. The light was beginning to fade.

Twilight plays strange tricks and at first Minerva thought she was imagining the tall figure who was standing so still in the middle of the lane, looking at her intently.

He removed his curly brimmed beaver with a flourish and swept her a low bow.

"Miss Armitage. Your very humble servant," he said.

Minerva stopped and stared, and stared again.

"Sylvester!" she screamed, and flew straight into his arms, as the lid of her work basket flew open and bobbins and silks and wool went flying over the frosty road.

Crying and laughing, she threw her arms around him, lips raised for his kiss.

He held her a little away from him, and she looked up into his eyes suddenly anxious.

"I love you, Minerva," he said in a husky voice. "Will

you do me the very great honour of giving me your hand in marriage?''

''Oh, yes,'' said the vicar's daughter, kissing him so passionately that he staggered slightly, and then wrapped his arms more tightly around her so that he could give back as good as he was getting.

''Minerva,'' he said thickly, freeing his mouth at last. ''We must be married very soon. I cannot wait.''

''Why wait?'' laughed Minerva.

''You are an abandoned hussy. A veritable jade. We shall behave like the respectable people we are and go home and tell your family the good news before I misbehave myself in this freezing lane. Kiss me again!''

It was quite half an hour before they walked dreamily into the vicarage to be welcomed by screams and exclamations from the girls. Mrs. Armitage was so overjoyed she forgot to have a Spasm.

Annabelle alone stood quietly in a corner of the room, watching Lord Sylvester, watching the love and laughter in his eyes and the beautiful curve of his mouth. The Marquess of Brabington turned from congratulating his friend and saw Annabelle, and a shadow crossed his face.

Soon they were all seated around the table in the vicarage dining room. London society would have been hard put to recognize the haughty Lord Sylvester as that gentleman sat with little Frederica on his knee, his face transfigured with happiness.

''I will always cherish that letter, my love,'' he said, smiling at Minerva over Frederica's curls.

''Oh, that terrible letter!'' cried Minerva.

''Not that one,'' he teased. ''The beautiful one that brought me here.''

Minerva's eyes opened wide. She opened her mouth to speak. ''More wine, my dear?'' said her father at her shoulder. She twisted her head and looked up at the vicar. His left eyelid drooped in a wink.

''Well, whatever brought my future son-in-law here, I am sure it was the work of God,'' said the vicar piously. ''Don't you think so, Minerva?''

''Oh, y-yes, Papa,'' faltered Minerva. ''Of course.''

And when she turned and saw the glowing love in Lord Sylvester's face, she forgot about everything else.

The merry company gathered in the drawing room after dinner. Quite flushed with wine and success, the vicar squeezed his wife's hand.

"Well, I think I arranged Minerva's marriage very well," he said complacently. "What a lot of hard work it was!"

"We must give praise where praise is due," said Mrs. Armitage. "You arranged Minerva's come-out to be sure, but you had no hand in bringing Lord Sylvester to Hopeworth to propose marriage."

"Eh, what?" For a moment the vicar was sorely tempted to tell his wife of how he and Squire Radford had put their heads together to plan a reconciliation. But Mrs. Armitage might tell, and worse, she might have one of her famous Spasms. So he contented himself by saying gruffly, "Aye, well, you have the right of it, ma'am. Now we have the other five to think of.

"Plaguey things, women," sighed the vicar of St. Charles and St. Jude. "*Demned* plaguey!"

About the Author

Marion Chesney was born in Glasgow, Scotland, where she began her successful writing career. She has worked as a fiction buyer, a theater critic, a newspaper journalist, a book reviewer, and a crime reporter.

She has been living in the United States since 1971. Most recently she has been writing full-time and living in Brooklyn with her author-husband and their child. Ms. Chesney is now hard at work on the adventures of Minerva's younger sisters.